Episode 10

Uneasy
Alliance

Elk Lake Publishing

Uneasy Alliance, Episode 10, In the President's Service

Copyright © 2016 by Ace Collins

Requests for information should be addressed to:

Elk Lake Publishing, Atlanta, GA 30024

ISBN-13 Number: 978-1-944430-00-9

Graphics Design: Anna M. O'Brien

Editor: Deb Haggerty

Published in Association with Hartline Literary Agency

In the President's Service Series:
Episode 10

Uneasy
Alliance

Elk Lake
PUBLISHING™

CHAPTER I

Friday, July 10, 1942
8:32 PM
Under the waters of the Atlantic

Henry Reese glanced over to the U-boat commander as he sipped on a cup of lukewarm tea. Still playing the role of Nigel Armstrong, the Brit who sold out his own country for a trunk filled with loot, the American had gotten to know the talkative Commander Fritz Klein very well over the past few days. He'd discovered the German, who spoke excellent English, had an affinity for American swing music and Hollywood actress Carole Landis and seemed to relish the visitor's company. Thus, when he was not on the con, Klein often invited Reese to his quarters where the two shared coffee, tea, crackers, and war news. Tonight that invite was once more given and accepted.

"Well," the host casually announced he sat on his small bunk and looked across to Reese occupying the tiny room's one chair, "our U-boats knocked out another half dozen ships yesterday. A South American merchant vessel is now resting not far from where I'll be dropping you off next week."

"So the war's going well," Reese announced in a clipped, English accent, pretending to be excited by the report that in truth made him sick to his stomach.

"The naval part of the war is going well," Klein corrected the visitor. "Those of us in the water are doing our part and doing it with effective gusto. Yet, from what I've been told, there are some troubles on the Eastern front. Russia is not the paper tiger many of the generals believed."

The visitor seemingly grew concerned. "So has Hitler bitten off more than he can chew?"

"Does it matter to you?" the sub commander asked.

"Not really," Reese's lie was in keeping with the part he was playing. "I have what I want; what happens next is not my concern. My hope is that at least for me this war is over. I want to lie out in the Mexican sun, get a tan and maybe learn to play guitar. Of course, I also want to meet some of the beautiful women I've heard live in this out of the way spot on the globe."

Klein, his skin pale from all his days away from the sun, nodded and wearily announced, "I guess you do. I think we'd all like to get away from it for a while. The quick victories we experienced in 1939 now seem decades ago."

The dark circles under the commander's eyes indicated he was tired and worn, but Klein also seemed much more relaxed and open than was usual for a military officer at war. Perhaps this was because, for a bit more than a week, this man with the reputation as one of his navy's greatest hunters had been given a reprieve. You could even call it a vacation. With Reese on board, the commander was not allowed to fight. Thus, Klein had not pursued the three British merchant vessels that had crossed their path or the American troop ship they'd spotted yesterday. In a very real sense, this was the journey of an underwater cruise ship that catered to only one passenger while the sub's men played cards, wrote letters home, read books, and listened to music.

So it almost seemed unnatural, as the two men sat in the commander's small quarters, surrounded by curved wood paneled walls, a few charts, family photos, and a half dozen books, that the German shifted the conversation to the war … something the two had avoided during their previous evening chats. And when he dove in, there was nothing reticent about his question. Like most men in his position, his query was blunt and his thoughts were fired off with the same deadly intent as torpedoes. Only this time, he wasn't demanding Reese justify his taste in books or music, he was searching for an answer much more haunting. Klein was no longer interested in his guest's cultural taste; he was challenging his character.

"How does it feel to sell out your country?"

Reese, falling into the guise of a conman/spy, had been prepared for that last verbal volley and didn't hesitate in answering. In fact, he was shocked the German had put that question off as long as he had.

Reese nodded and forced a smile as he looked directly into Klein's blue eyes. "I expected that question when I climbed aboard." He paused, licking his lips for effect, before asking, "What took you so long? Why did we have to go through several nights of discussing a myriad of things that didn't matter to get to the one thing that's most important to you and millions of others? Since the moment you drew this assignment, you have been dying to know to know and understand why I jolly well sold out King and country."

"I'm not attacking you," Klein shot back as he pulled on the neck of this turtleneck shirt, "after all, you're providing vital information to us so that makes you a type of dark hero to the Fatherland. I just wanted to know why you chose the route you did? Why was it so easy to not just turn your back on the Union Jack but run the banner down the flag pole and sell it."

In truth, Reese wondered the same thing. Why had Armstrong sold out? What had been the Englishman's motivation? He really had no idea. In fact, he couldn't imagine it. But he had to answer so what lie would he pull out of his hat?

Putting himself into the spy's shoes, he shrugged and imagined a few fictional reasons for this act of treason. The first thing that popped into his head was that the guy was tired of dodging bombs. Then another thought came to him; maybe he had been seduced by Hitler's views on Aryan supremacy. Yet, as

Reese weighed those two theories, something far more central to the human situation began to take shape. Armstrong was likely just a lonely man who wanted wealth and figured, with no real options to achieve that dream, selling information was his only way to get it. Building on the thought of a loser looking for a way to appear like a winner, Reese launched his carefully measured response.

"Wars are fought for territory and money. Those who start the wars sit in their palaces and push the commoners out to die. So I ask you, why should the blokes in charge be the only ones who profit? Why shouldn't we get a piece of the action? After all it's the poor man who carries the load and often dies for something he doesn't understand. I was just tired to being the poor man and tired of seeing my friends who were poor die because they weren't born with blue blood. I did what I did for them as well as me. The life I will live will be for Freddie, Herman, John, and Andrew."

"Who are they?"

"My friends I went to school with. The ones I played darts with. The chums who I shared dreams with. And the four who marched off to war and didn't come back."

The story was a lie, but Reese was well aware that it might as well have been true. Scores watched their friends die every day and most of those whose blood mixed with the mud in the trenches were from the poor sides of towns.

"Your point," the sub commander solemnly replied, "is well taken." The short, thin man then frowned as he took a final swig from his cup. After letting the foul tasting liquid slip down his throat, he glanced over to a calendar. His eyes lingered there for several seconds before he turned back to his guest and said, "But if everyone felt as you did there would be no order and the world would dissolve into chaos."

Reese laughed, "Look around you; chaos is everywhere. The world is on fire, millions are screaming for mercy while others are shooting their brains out and you believe that is order?"

"Okay," Klein admitted, "it might look like chaos right now, but war is fought to bring order to the world."

"So, war is fought to bring peace?" Reese laughed. "There's more irony in that thought than any I've heard for a long time."

For a moment, the confident man almost looked perplexed. He glanced nervously from his guest to a photo that must have been his family and then to the ceiling. When he did finally did speak, his gaze did not immediately return to Reese.

"Until a few months ago, I though I fully understood war and my place in it. I saw what we were doing as clearly as if it had been ordained by God. But now I'm not so sure."

A suddenly fascinated Reese nodded and asked, "What changed your mind?"

"Believe it or not," Klein cracked, "it was the man who made you rich!"

"Hitler?"

"Yeah."

For a few seconds, both men went mute. Reese had no idea what why the commander was holding his tongue, but he was deeply intrigued by the mere thought a German seemed to almost be questioning the Fuhrer. He was still trying to come to grips with that realization and find a way to exploit it when Klein's voice again filled the small cabin.

"Mr. Armstrong, let me pose a question. What happened on December 7, 1941?"

Reese shrugged, "I wish my history teachers had given pop quizzes that were so easy to answer. My marks would have been far better in school."

"Naturally," Klein casually noted, "you think I'm talking about the Japanese bombing of Pearl Harbor."

"Well," the American still pretending to be a Brit cut in, "that was the big news that day. The Yanks got pretty balled up about it."

The German stood, pulled his uniform jacket off, tossed it onto his bunk and sighed. "A few thousand lives were taken in a sneak attack and suddenly there is no longer a regional war. Instead, it has become a world war. And maybe that's how December 7th will always be remembered. But there was something else that happened that day, something that no one is writing about and only a few have heard of, and it might even shock you and the world far more than the Japs shocked FDR on that Sunday morning in the Pacific." He leaned back, the look on his face indicating he now was questioning sharing what was obviously on his mind but, even if he doubted if it was the wise thing to do, the German resolutely marched forward. "I can assure you that a December event, cloaked in shadows and only whispered of in a few back rooms at the Reichstag, was far more deadly and its long-term implications much more dangerous than what happened in Hawaii."

"That's hard to believe," a now completely confused Reese replied.

"No, my friend, it is not." The commander paused and looked into Reese's cup. "Would you like some more tea?"

"No, I had to choke down the first cup."

Klein grinned, "I'm not sure there is a such a thing as a good cup of tea. But you English people seem to thrive on it."

"I'm more of a Coca-Cola man myself," came the quick reply. "Now, pushing beyond my personal taste in beverages, let's get back to what you just tossed out. If Pearl Harbor dragging the Americans into the war was not the most important event on that day, then what do you feel was so significant about December 7th? Why does that day seemingly haunt you?"

"It's a long story," Klein suggested, "one that sounds more like fiction that reality."

"Are you going to share it," the American asked, "or are you just going to tease me?"

"Other than my brother who is on the general staff," he explained, "I've never told anyone about December 7th. I probably shouldn't have even brought it up now. It's a tale better left untold."

"Typical German," Reese grumbled, "you brag about things, but you never explain them."

"Is that the way we are?" Klein asked with a smile.

"Well, the man at the top is certainly that way," the American explained. His curiosity aroused, Reese pushed for information. "You've got nothing to lose in telling me a story. I mean it's not like I can run down the hallway and alert anyone on this ship. I'm an outsider here and, as a man who sold out his country, will be one of the rest of my life no matter where I go. On top of that, I'm trying to get away from the war, not be a part of it."

"Maybe you're right," the U-Boat commander announced with a nod, "but God knows I'm really only sharing this because I need to tell someone. Just knowing what I now has become very much a cancer killing me one piece at a time."

"Okay," Reese barked, "I'll be your sounding board, but please just get to it. I'm not a man who enjoys dragging things out."

Klein nodded. "Okay, but I warn you, this might keep you awake too. For starters, let me take you back to my December 7th. That was the day when I rethought the war and my place in it. I wasn't on duty that day. In fact, I wasn't even on the water. My boat was undergoing repairs and, during my shore leave, I was invited to meet with Hitler himself. It seems the Fuhrer wanted a chance to have a one-on-one conversation with the Great Klein … the Sea Shark as he called me." The commander shook his head and grimly offered a pointed observation. "I've found that during war being an effective killer opens the doors everywhere except to a prison. Now you talk about irony!" After allowing his thoughts to momentarily linger in the air, he pushed on with his story. "On that winter's day, after pinning a medal on my chest, our glorious leader began to brag about the many accomplishments of the Nazi war machine." The commander suddenly lowered his voice to a whisper. "During our fifteen-minute conversation, he let something slip I was never supposed to know. What he shared that day has been haunting me ever since."

Klein swept his hand through his thinning blonde hair and grew silent. Staring once more at the calendar, his blue eyes closed until they were nothing more than slits. For the moment, he seemed like a man suffering a numbing type of pain brought on by an unseen disease. What was eating at him? Reese wanted to know but also figured he couldn't push too hard or the commander would clam up. So he impatiently waited. Finally, after several minutes during which only the sounds of the submarine's engines kept the room from a seeming like a tomb, the host glanced back to his guest and shrugged. "I've gotten to know you too well too quickly on this trip. For a second, I almost shared things I would not even tell my wife."

"I understand," Reese announced, his stoic reply masking his deep interest and his impatience to find out what was so troubling to the U-boat commander.

What was the best way to keep the story going? The American figured prodding wasn't it, but what was? Maybe it was time to give his host a break. Maybe it was the right moment to appeal to his pride. Thus, when the American spoke, he moved the conversation in that direction.

"As you struggle with your thoughts, perhaps now it's time for an observation of mine."

"Which is?"

"You're a man who loves what he does."

"Ah," Klein noted with a smile, "the game of war. I was made for this life. I love stalking the prey and then eluding the enemy when he stalks me. There is an exhilaration in watching a ship go down and knowing it was by my hand that it sank. The boiling of the sea when a vessel slips beneath the waves brings satisfaction like nothing you can begin to imagine. So yes, I love to watch the explosion caused by my torpedoes and I relish that destruction." He formed his right hand into a first and snarled, "There is nothing like that sense of power!"

"I figured as much," Reese cracked. "And if Hitler wanted to see you … to honor the shark … then you must have a lot of kills. So I guess you have felt the rush of victory many times."

The commander nodded. "In the last year and a half, I've sunk more than forty ships. Imagine that for a moment. There are more than forty rusting hulks resting on the ocean floor and they are there because of my cunning and skills."

Reese nodded. "That's an impressive record. After getting to know you and sensing your great pride, I'll bet you can recall each of your scores."

"By name, country, and tonnage," the commander bragged.

"And how many people have you killed?" Reese coldly asked.

"I sink ships," Klein shot back. "That's my job."

"But people are on those ships," the guest argued, "Those people have families and dreams. They didn't ask for war or start it. Most aren't even in uniform. So don't their deaths mean anything to you?"

As the smile left his lips, the commander once more grew silent. Glancing back to his calendar, he folded his hands together and moved one thumb over the other. After an uncomfortable sixty seconds, he looked back to his guest. "Have you ever killed a man?"

"Yes," came the quick reply. Realizing he'd answered as Henry Reese and not Nigel Armstrong, he paused to find a way to logically justify his response. He finally regained his footing by asking, "How much do you know about me?"

"Only that you have information Hitler wants," Klein announced, "and I am supposed to take you to wherever you want to go."

Relieved, the American crafted a tale that was fact mixed with fiction. "I wasn't always a spy; I've been in combat. I've seen men die as I shot or stabbed them. I've even gone through their pockets and found the letters they'd gotten from home and seen pictures of their loved ones. And those images haunt me." He paused, licked his drying lips before coldly suggesting, "I think death doesn't haunt you because you kill from distance. You don't hear their last gasps or put your hand in their warm blood. To you it's about tonnage but to me it's about people. I didn't kill soulless metal ships; I killed real, breathing human beings."

"So you sold out because you got tired of the blood?" Klein asked.

"I'm tired of the blood," Reese admitted, now speaking fully as himself rather than as Nigel Armstrong.

"And so," Klein noted, "You profit from the death you loathe rather than actually getting involved in the fight."

"Is that so bad?" the American asked.

"Maybe not," the German admitted. "A part of me would like to get off this sub with you and walk away from the war."

"But you enjoy it so," Reese noted.

"Maybe I did," Klein cracked, "but that all started to change on December 7th."

"So," the American asked, "we are back to what you so badly want to talk about but can't." He studied his host's face. Suddenly, he seemed to have aged a decade. Sensing he was ready to open up, Reese moved in for the verbal kill. "I was honest with you about my feelings about the blood on my hands, now it's time for you to be the same. Why was the passion for the game of war snuffed out then?"

"Blood on your hands," the German cracked. "You call that being honest? Millions have blood on their hands."

"I told you what was in my gut," Reese shot back, "now what's boiling in yours? Something's eating on you, what is it?"

The commander shook his head. "I guess it won't hurt to share the information with a man soon to be hiding from both sides. I mean who would believe a piece of sea sludge who's sold out his country for thirty pieces of silver?"

"If that was supposed to sting," Reese shot back, "it didn't.

17

And I'm getting a lot more than thirty pieces of silver."

"Yes, you are," Klein agreed. "And you are by the far the most intelligent person in this tin can right now so I'll guess I'll illuminate you to what this war is really all about. When I'm finished, you'll realize that what happened at Pearl Harbor is like pricking a dying man with a pin when compared to my December 7th."

"I'm not sure you can sell me on that one," the American jabbed. "No matter what your explosive information is, I just don't believe it can top the Jap's sneak attack. As I see it, getting the Yanks into the war was the biggest news since Germany rolled into Russia."

"Okay, Mr. Armstrong, if that's what you believe then strap yourself down because this bit of secret information will make you sick to your stomach." Klein then pointed a finger in his guest's face. "I don't care if you are a traitor. What I tell you will haunt your nights and constantly invade your days. In fact, it might just keep you from ever enjoying that loot you treasured more than loyalty to your country. So are you sure you want to hear it?"

"Absolutely."

"On December 7th," Klein solemnly announced, now seemingly anxious to spill his guts, "a giddy Hitler told me a special camp was opening in Poland that would take care of the real reason for world suffering."

"A camp?" Reese asked. "You mean like one of those German youth camps I've heard about where they warp the minds of impressionable teens into believing Hitler's a god?"

"If only it was that innocent." Reaching over to the tiny, built-in desk, Klein pulled out a five by seven-inch photo. He glanced at it for a moment before handing it to his guest.

"What do you see?" the commander demanded.

The German's stare was so intense it took Reese a few seconds to turn his eyes from the man to the photo. The image captured on the piece of paper was both confusing and unsettling. It showed about fifty nude women of all ages walking across snow covered ground with uniformed armed guards apparently urging them forward.

"So this is the camp?" Reese asked still trying to figure out what was going on and why he'd been handed the photo.

"Yes," Klein whispered, "my half-brother gave me that photo. He was actually proud of taking it. He was there on December 7th, the day we Nazis started using that camp to euthanize Jews."

"What do you mean euthanize?" the stunned American demanded.

"Cold-blooded, industrial-type execution! And I don't mean just a few business leaders or traitors; I'm talking men, women, and children. Let me make this even more clear … we are killing everyone from grandmothers to babies. Even tonight, at this very moment, we are loading them onto trains like cattle, shipping them to this camp, stripping them, pushing them into a room and gassing them like unwanted mongrel dogs. Those women in the photo were some of the first to smell the poisonous fumes that snuffed out their lives and have been snuffing out lives ever since December 7th. How did the American president put it?— 'A day that will live in infamy.' He had no idea how universally that statement described December 7, 1941."

Reese remained silent as he tried to understand just what he'd been told. Meanwhile, Klein, his eyes now moist, rubbed his lips and took the photo back. After shoving it into the desk drawer, he added, "The number we killed in that camp on December 7th dwarfs the number the Americans lost at Pearl Harbor."

"You're serious?"

"Dead serious," the commander quickly shot back. "And this extermination won't end until we have rounded up every Jew in Europe. We are even building more camps so we can do the job quicker and better."

"I don't know what to say?"

"There is nothing to say," Klein quickly explained. "Last December 11th, Hitler declared war on the United States. I don't think he did it because he wanted to honor his treaty with Japan; I believe he made that stupid move because, in his mind, the Jews control the policies and the business in the United States. He has become so self-consumed with the Jews he has lost all reason. I guess to him, it is always about the Jews. In his mind, it is personal. He believes the Jews are out to get him, to bring him down, and they are the reason Germany has been held back."

The commander glanced at his watch. "I need to get back to the con."

"Before you go," Reese cut in, "I need to know something."

"What?"

"What are your feelings for the Jews? I can understand this upsetting someone like me, who has so many Jewish friends, but if you're a Nazi, why does it bother you? Aren't you marching lockstep with Hitler?"

"That's not an easy question to answer," Klein admitted. "After all, most of the military leaders and those in the Nazi party have come to see the Jews as nothing more than dogs. But for me, there's more to it." He paused, shook his head and frowned. "Perhaps you will understand my convoluted emotions if I share something which only a handful of trusted friends know. You see, I have gone to great lengths over the past decade to hide the fact my mother was actually Jewish."

"How did you keep that a secret?" Reese asked.

"My parents were divorced when I was five and my father made sure everyone believed his second wife was my mother. He even had my birth certificate altered."

"And your real mother?"

"My friend, I quietly kept up with her until last year. It seems that on December 5th, she was taken from her home in Berlin and pushed onto a train bound for Treblinka, Poland."

"So she's …"

"I'm sure," came the quiet reply, "along with hundreds of thousands of others, she suffered the same fate as those women marching across the snow. In fact, she might have one of them. Now it's my turn to ask you a question."

"Shoot."

"You've made you decision, you have found a way to get out of this war, but what would you do if you were me?"

"I don't know," Reese admitted.

"My father's family is completely loyal to the Nazi goals," Klein explained. "They march blindly to Hitler's orders. But on December 7th, something I should have realized years ago dawned on me. Hitler's hate for Jews is so strong, it has overruled his common sense. His hate is, therefore, suicidal. When the world finds out about his passion to destroy an entire race of people, the nations will come together as one and level us. The Allies will not rest until every German is brought to their knees in shame."

"That will happen even if the word doesn't get out," the American suggested. "In time, Hitler will be defeated."

"Not before millions of innocent men, women, and children have died in those camps."

"So," Reese asked, "does that mean you will continue to hunt prey? Does that mean you will prolong this war and in the process buy even more time for your mother's people to be murdered?"

"Now you know why I have problems sleeping," Klein cracked. "You see, I'm like the rat in the trap; there is no way out. Now, if you will excuse me, I need to check with my crew and make sure we are pushing toward your destination point." He shrugged, "I envy you, Nigel; you'll be walking away from all the things that are eating me alive."

The American silently stood and followed Klein out of the room and down the narrow hall. A few steps brought the American to his assigned quarters. Climbing into his bunk, he closed his eyes and tried to assimilate what he'd just learned. If the commander was right, and that photograph seemed to indicate he was, then this war was far worse than anyone in the states could imagine.

CHAPTER 2

Sunday, July 12, 1942
9:16 AM
Team Headquarters outside of Drury, Maryland

Even by Maryland standards it was a hot summer morning; making it seem all the worse was high humidity and lack of a breeze. Standing on the front porch of the large brick home serving as her team's headquarters, Helen Meeker looked down the long lane toward the yellow 1936 Packard sedan slowly moving toward her. She knew her sister Alison was behind the wheel, but it was the passenger who held her interest. For reasons unknown and so far unexplained, the President had assigned a British woman to accompany the team on a mission that had not yet been fully defined. Being given Dizzy Vance had pushed Meeker's patience to its limits and this move took it well beyond that. It was well past time for her to make a clandestine trip to the capitol and have a face to face with the man in charge.

As it rolled slowly toward the house, Alison eased the touring sedan to a stop directly in front of Meeker's position. Before the driver had switched off the key, the visitor stepped out. Not surprising! After all, she was British and they always seemed to be prompt. This unwanted addition to their club was bit over five-five though the brown heels she was wearing added at least two inches to that height. The woman's fair skin glowed in the morning sun revealing a dusting of freckles; her hair and eyes were dark, her face attractive but showing no emotion, and she was dressed in a form-fitting tan suit and matching hat. She looked so prim and conservative Meeker wondered if the woman had borrowed the outfit from the queen herself.

"I'm guessing you are Helen," the visitor announced with a very proper British accent. "I've heard some very remarkable things about you."

Meeker nodded. "Well, you are way ahead of me; I've heard nothing about you." As the newcomer closed the distance between them, Meeker coldly inquired, "So what brings you across the pond?"

Extending her gloved hand, the woman smiled. "I'm here to help you unwrap a Christmas present or at least that's what the mission is designated ... Christmas in July is what it's been dubbed."

"That's the scoop," Alison announced as she joined the other two on the porch. "The chief said St. Nick is coming south of the border and bringing in something really swell."

After shaking the visitor's hand, Meeker looked back to her sister. "Are you supposed to make the introductions?"

"I can handle that," the visitor cut in. "I really don't need my charming driver's help. I'm Sergeant Gail Worel of the Women's Auxiliary Air Force. I was an aid assigned to Russell Strickland before being asked to come to the states and work with you on this mission."

"I see," Meeker coolly replied. After raising her right eyebrow, she added, "And why is it my team needs help? We've done pretty well on our own."

"I'm afraid a part of it's classified," Worel explained, "but I can tell you this. The package that's being brought on the U-boat contains something that was stolen a few years ago from the Crown. My government wants to get it back."

"So," Meeker suggested, "it is a part of the war effort?"

"No," the visitor answered, "it's a part of history."

"And that's all there is to this surreptitious operation?"

"Not exactly," Worel explained, "the man bringing that item is an important cog in the European underground and …" She paused, suddenly losing a bit of her English reserve, bit her lip and softly added, "And perhaps a man I might could love."

"So," Meeker announced with a frown, "I'm a matchmaker now. I'm going to be the guide who reunites Bogart and Bergman?"

"I don't understand," Worel cut in.

"It's a flick," Alison cut in, "set in Africa where the hero picks service to country over his heartthrob."

"Casablanca?" Worel asked.

"You've seen it?" Alison asked.

25

"Hasn't everyone?" came the reply. "No, you've got me wrong. I'm here strictly for the item not to stir up old emotions. My country doesn't send its people halfway around the world for romance but, I'll be honest, I'm looking forward to the reunion."

"Do you have any bags?" Meeker asked, her tone still showing her frustration in having someone else added to her team and that someone coming in with a schoolgirl crush.

"I'll get them," Alison announced, "then I'm scooting off to the star city. Going to whirl a bit with a Hoosier before digging some bad notes at a jive joint."

Worel and Meeker both jerked their heads toward the younger women and in unison asked, "What?"

"Shake it from your skull," Alison answered. "What I'm yelping is way beyond your wavelength."

"Yeah," Meeker groaned. "Sergeant Worel …"

"Gail."

"Okay, Gail. Follow me and I'll give you a look at our home and headquarters."

Five minutes later, after a cook's tour and Alison's departure, the women made their way into the study. Sitting opposite each other in low-backed Victorian chairs, Meeker sipping on a six-ounce Coke in a bottle and Worel drinking hot tea, they both seem to relax for the first time. The visitor was the one who lobbed the observation that served as a real icebreaker.

"I have no idea what your sister was talking about. I stayed confused from the moment we met until she left. Guess I've got a lot to learn about American English."

Meeker grinned. "If you do, then I do as well. Alison's generation speaks a tongue all their own. Fortunately, Becca Bobbs, my right hand on this team, can translate when needed. Enough about Alison, I hope you had a good trip."

"It was fine," she assured her host. "Flying is a part of my training and my life. I have no problems sleeping even on a transport. So I'm actually pretty well rested."

"Do you need something to eat?"

"No, your sister took care of that. But I'm guessing you'd like a bit more information on the mission."

"You guessed right."

"About five years ago while on display with other items at an Irish exhibit, three of the crown jewels disappeared. The items included a ring, a necklace, and a bracelet that were over three hundred years old. While they serve no real purpose to the war effort, the fact that Hitler had possession of them did grate on the royal nerves. As a part of the deal to sell out an important member of the underground, Nigel Armstrong, a bumbling spy, demanded those three items along with cash, gold, and diamonds."

"And Armstrong is going to give them to us?" Meeker inquired. "That's the kind of service I don't normally see out of spies."

"No," Worel assured her host, "in fact, Armstrong is in a British prison under heavy guard. One of our people, an American pretending to be Armstrong, took his place. Right now he has the loot and is on a U-boat bringing him to a spot off the Mexican coast. He's due to arrive in about six to ten days. We will get a message detailing exactly when and where."

"And, if you don't mind me asking, why are the Germans offering this underwater delivery service?"

"Because they think once Armstrong is safely on shore, he will give them the name of Europe's most effective underground leader … a man Hitler calls the Shadow of Night. Of course, the information he will share will be a ruse."

There was irony; Hitler was willing to pay a fortune for something Meeker already knew. Hans Holsclaw, a man she'd worked with, a man who'd seen Henry Reese die, was the underground leader. Yet, while this information proved interesting, the case still didn't sound like a project that needed their kind of expertise. After all, they had a lot of other things on their plates at the moment. There had to be more to it but could she get the British bird to spill the beans?

"So the jewels are all this is about?" Meeker asked. "I'd figure in times of war they wouldn't matter that much."

"No," Worel assured her. "The jewels are the Christmas present we want but, now we're alone, I can tell you the real mission is to kidnap the sub's commander. Fritz Klein is the most effective killer in the Nazi navy. He's also one of the most important living symbols of their military. To grab him would serve to upset the man with the mustache more than you can imagine. And getting the U-boat along with Klein would be a huge bonus."

"So," Helen opined, "even as good as my team is, to arranged an attack and grab the sub when they are dropping off the man pretending to be a spy … well … that sounds like too big a job for the four of us plus you."

"Actually," the guest explained, "if all goes well, our man will disable the sub and we will be able to take it ourselves."

"Still," Meeker noted, "and this time, let me see if I can make this clear to you. There are not going to be that many of us."

"Won't have to be," she confidently answered, "our man is that good. The sub won't run, there will only be a few men in the landing party, we grab those blokes, secure them, then radio the US Army and Navy. While we are getting away, they will grab the sub. And the best part about all of this is your cover will not be blown."

The plan now sounded solid, but there was an aspect of the whole affair that had Meeker confused. Why was her team needed? This seemed like a job a small group from the Coast Guard could handle. Turning her gaze back to her guest, Meeker made an observation.

"Gail, you don't need us. You've got a plan that can be carried out by a small military unit much better than it can by my team."

"Helen, you might be right, but there is a very good reason you're needed. I wouldn't be here if that weren't the case."

Like a bolt out of the blue, it hit Meeker. The team's involvement wasn't about the U-boat, the commander, or the jewels, so it must be the only other element in the puzzle.

"Gail, you must need us to help you with your man."

"He's as far undercover as you are," the visitor explained. "We can't reveal his identity even to your military. We have to protect him."

"He must be special," Meeker noted.

29

"He's like no one I've ever met," Worel assured her. "He melted my British reserve faster than you can fathom. Though we didn't get to spend too much time together, we did share a few days before the sub picked him up. In those hours, he touched places no one has ever touched. He got me to share things I'd never shared. When I said a final goodbye to him as he prepared to row out to the meeting point with the U-boat, I thought I was going to die. I didn't want to let him go. I still feel that last kiss. Do you know what that's like?"

"Actually," Meeker sadly admitted, "I do. But if things work as planned, you'll get your man back. I watched the man I should have loved die and I never got the chance to tell him how I really felt."

"So sorry."

"It was my fault," Meeker admitted. "And it haunts me every day."

"Helen, as much as that man quickly coming back means to me, he means much more to the Allied General Command. He's the best we have. In fact, he's the right hand man to the Shadow of Night."

Who knew Americans were regulars in the underground? Meeker was about to ask Worel to share a bit more about the man who was at the heart of this new mission when Becca Bobbs rushed in.

"Nice outfit," Meeker noted.

Bobbs, her blonde hair pulled back in a ponytail and dressed in paint-splattered blue pants and pullover blouse, frowned. "I was working on a cabinet in my lab."

"Yeah, I can see that it's going well."

"The paint can's lid was stuck. When I finally pried it open, it spattered a bit."

Meeker grinned, "I like the new highlights in your hair. Now, what pulled you away from vital war work?"

"We've got a job," Bobbs announced. Noticing Worel for the first time she added, "And you must be our guest from England."

Meeker stood, "This is Sergeant Gail Worel of the Women's Air Force. Gail, this is the woman of many talents

whose most important one is translating what Alison says. Her name is Becca Bobbs."

The guest nodded toward Bobbs before the blonde continued, "We have an assignment that needs to be finished before we head to Mexico."

"You already know about that?" Meeker asked.

"Alison dropped by my lab and told me. Anyway, before we take our Mexican vacation, another less exotic trip has been dropped into our laps. It seems a general's wife is missing. The White House doesn't want the press to find out so they are keeping the FBI out of this and that's why it falls to us."

"Which general?" Meeker demanded.

"Jefferson Root. He's assigned to the Pentagon right now."

"He's got three stars too," Meeker noted. "What do we know?"

"We are on our way to Taylorville, Illinois," Bobb's explained. "That's not far from Springfield. A friend of the family spotted Mrs. Root in a hotel there but when she called out, the woman didn't acknowledge her."

The team leader smiled grimly, "Okay, let's get packed and ready to move. Before we leave, I want photos of the woman, a complete breakdown of her life and her relationship with her husband. Call Clay in from Arkansas. We'll need him to fly us to our location and help us with the groundwork. And he needs to find us a place where we can land, set up our headquarters and not be noticed."

"What about Dizzy?" Bobbs asked.

"We won't need him," Meeker announced. "Finding a missing woman shouldn't be that hard. Plus, he needs to do a bit more bonding with Miss Boatright in Warm Springs."

"What about me?" Worel asked.

"You better go with us," Meeker suggested. "If this takes too long, we'll have to leave from that location to go to Mexico. Besides, as Becca, Clay, and I are all supposed to be dead, it might prove handy to have someone who's not a ghost in case we need to visit with the local law. So, if you have your uniform, bring it. Uniforms always impress small town cops … especially when they are being modeled by someone who looks like Vivian Leigh. Now we likely only have a few hours to do our homework before we leave, so let's do some digging. What's the woman's first name?"

"Gertrude," Bobbs announced.

"I wonder what kind of woman she is?" Meeker asked. "Better yet, I wonder if she ran away or if someone kidnapped here? Either way this is likely going to be unpleasant. Becca, run down the old friend who spotted her in …

"Taylorville."

"Yeah, that's it. She'll be the first person we'll want to meet with." Meeker turned to Worel. "You are about to get a tour of America's heartland. I hope you enjoy knee-high corn, hogs, tractors, and hot, humid weather."

"Sounds ducky. I'll make sure I have lots of film for my camera."

CHAPTER 3

Monday, July 13, 1942
8:35 AM
The Diamond Café, Taylorville, Illinois

True to its name, the Diamond Café embraced a baseball theme. The walls were decorated with photos of local and professional players, there were autographed balls in cases behind the long counter, and bats hanging from the walls. The menus were shaped like a ballpark and beneath the food choices were screened images of bases, a plate, and a pitcher's mound. It was more than obvious someone in the joint loved America's favorite pastime.

After entering the Main Street restaurant's glass door, the four visitors moved to a round table in the back and ordered the grand slam breakfast special. They'd just finished their meal of pancakes, scrambled eggs, and bacon when they were joined by a woman about fifty-five dressed in a print summer dress, low pumps, and a stylish hat. Her short red hair was freshly styled and, though it was early in the morning, she was sporting full make-up including the brightest lipstick Meeker had ever seen. The guest was plump but attractive and the minute she opened her mouth, she proved she was also assured and confident.

"So you probably don't believe I saw Gertie," she began as she took a chair between Bobbs and Barnes. "You probably think I'm crazy and just looking for attention. That's what most folks believe about women my age who aren't married. Everyone seems to believe we just crave the spotlight and will do anything to saddle up to a single man. Well, that's not the case. I'm not hitched because that's the way I like it. I've had plenty of opportunities, but none of them met my standards." She glanced over to Barnes, smiled, flashed her blue eyes almost hidden under the false eyelashes, and asked, "How old are you, dearie?"

"He prefers blondes," Bobbs quipped, "and before we get started, are you Constance Rider? If not, we're likely wasting your time."

Her eyes still lingering on Barnes, the woman nodded. "I'm Miss Rider and I had no problem figuring out you were the folks who called and made the appointment."

"And why's that?" Meeker inquired.

Rider's eyes were still locked on Barnes as she answered. "Because I know everyone else in this place." She then glanced across to Bobbs, "And whatever you do, stay away from the eggs—they're powdered and they taste like cardboard."

"I'll bet nothing in here is as fresh as you are," Bobbs snapped.

"What do you mean by that?" Rider demanded.

Though she found the two women sparring over Barnes interesting, Meeker lightly tapped the table with her spoon and steered the conversation in a new direction. "Miss Rider, we've eaten and we've already made the mistake on the eggs. Now, we need to talk to you about where you saw Gertrude Root."

"Yeah, that," came the reply as the woman continued to glare at Bobbs.

"Go ahead and tell us about it," Meeker suggested. "I guess the first thing we need to know is why you felt a need to contact General Root."

"I called her husband's office yesterday," she explained, her eyes once again directed toward the only man at the table. "You see, I thought he should know Gertie was out from under his thumb again." Rider slowly moved her gaze from the man back to Meeker. "Don't get me wrong, Jeff's not the controlling type. I know because we dated in college, but he tries to keep that woman on a short lease. He should. Gertie was a tramp when we were in school and likely still is. You get a drink or two in her and she is liable to do and say anything."

Meeker nodded. The file they'd been given on Gertrude Root hinted she was not a Sunday school teacher and enjoyed the company of men more than she did attending hen club meetings. Yet from what Helen'd read, since marrying the general she hadn't taken any of the relationships to the affair level. Also, their notes indicated she was not really much of a drinker. So

Rider's observations were likely tainted by the fact she'd lost Jefferson Root to Gertrude thirty years before. Realizing now she'd have to weigh everything the woman said, Helen charged forward.

"Where did you see her?" Meeker asked.

For a moment, her eyes once more locked on Barnes, Rider seemed lost but just about the time Meeker was going to repeat the question, the woman found her voice. Still her gaze never left the now obviously uncomfortable man.

"She was coming out of the hotel at the end of the block. I was just leaving the beauty shop and I yelled, but she ignored me. She got into a dark Oldsmobile driven by a man I'd never seen ... so he wasn't a local ... and they drove off. Might I add, they were sitting pretty close together."

"What's the name of the hotel?" Bobbs cut in.

"The City Hotel. Matt and Clair Johnson used to run it, but a new manager came in a week ago. I heard someone from St. Louis bought it. Anyway, the place has a dozen rooms and each has a bath as well as plenty of bugs. You wouldn't want to stay there. In fact, I wouldn't be caught dead in there but it's likely Gertie's cup of tea."

Meeker had noted the brick, two-story building housing the hotel when they drove into town. From the outside it looked respectable, so once again Rider was likely stretching the truth.

"Miss Rider," the team leader continued, "Did Mrs. Root look distressed in any way?"

"No. She actually seemed like she was completely in control. Her nose was as high and proud as it always has been. She's always thought she was the blue hen's chick. I always saw her more as the sow's fat daughter myself."

"Have you seen her since?" Bobbs prodded.

"No. I only called Jeff because I wanted him to know that his wife was playing around on him with a tall, dark stranger." The woman glanced to Worel, "Did anyone ever tell you that you look like the woman who played Scarlett in *Gone With The Wind*?"

"Yes, I get that a lot."

"You even sound a bit like her," Rider added. "You're not from around her are you?"

"No," Worel admitted, "I'm from back east."

"Way back east," Bobbs added.

"So you didn't see Mrs. Root after that?" Meeker asked.

"No, I didn't.

"We appreciate your information. It has been helpful. Now we need to see if we can take what you gave us and find Mrs. Root."

"Not sure why anyone would want to find her," Rider snapped. "Jeff would be better off if Gertie stepped in front of an Illinois Central freight train. Now, I have dress fitting." As she pushed back from the table and stood, she glanced again toward Barnes. "If you're in town tonight and want someone to show you around, I own the two-story yellow house at 204 Elm. Just ring the bell, I'll be ready."

"Thanks," the man replied, "I'll make a note of that, but I figure we'll be gone by then."

The quartet of visitors watched Rider seductively wiggle her way out of the café before Bobbs noted, "That walk was all for you, Clay."

"Yeah," he groaned as he pulled at his shirt collar, "and I'd prefer not being here tonight. She's on the prowl."

Meeker nodded. "Don't worry about her; we need to chase down Gertrude Root. Clay, why don't you walk down the street and see if you can come up with anything at the hotel? Find out if she stayed at the place or anyone saw her visit someone there. We'll meet you out at our rental car."

As the man went to work, Meeker glanced around the restaurant. It was hard to believe a war was going on and that millions of Americans were fighting it on two fronts. The folks eating their morning meals acted as if nothing was amiss at all.

"What's on your mind?" Bobbs asked.

"Contrast. All around us folks are talking about the same things they did last year and the year before and the year before that. The world's upside down and their lives haven't changed."

"In spite of the bombing," Worel chimed in, "it's the same in England. You have to cling to whatever normal life you can find. If you don't, then the sense of knowing your loved ones might just die today in a place you couldn't find on the map will crush you."

"Yeah," Meeker nodded. "Maybe it's good we have something else to focus on too. So let's forget about the war and find our lost Gertie."

Getting up and wandering past a dozen tables to the front of the café, Helen paid the bill. She then led the other two women over to their light blue 1939 Ford sedan. Bobbs leaned against the front fender and studied the town while Worel reached into the car, pulled out a small Brownie camera and played the tourist game. After taking two photos of the street, she waved to Meeker.

"Why don't you and Becca stand in front of the car and I'll get a shot of you with the town in the background. I kind of want my friends back home to see what a small American village looks like when decorated by typical Yank women."

"What does that mean?" Bobbs teased. "There's nothing typical about Helen or me."

"It proves what most Brits think," Worel explained, "that everyone here looks like a movie star."

"Humor her," Meeker suggested, "it's a great way to kill time while Clay gets the information we need."

Three minutes and four photographs later, Barnes ambled up to the trio. After posing for what Worel called a final "snap," he leaned close to Meeker and delivered his report.

"Root and a tall man were at the hotel, but they only asked about a guest. The woman they inquired about was not due in until last night, so they left. The clerk isn't on duty after six so he doesn't know if they returned. He did hear the driver say they might as well go on to Springfield."

"What was the name of the woman they were looking for?" Meeker asked.

"Brown."

"What's next?" Bobbs asked.

41

"We need to talk to Miss Brown," Meeker suggested, "and see how she knows Root."

"I had the clerk called her room," Barnes volunteered, "and there was no answer."

As Meeker considered her options, Worel set her camera on the Ford's hood and studied something in the shadows of an alley. A moment later the Brit whispered, "In the King's name," and raced out into the street.

"Look out," Bobbs screamed as a ton and half truck filled with hogs headed directly toward the woman. If she heard the warning, Worel didn't acknowledge it, she just kept running. The truck missed her, but a Graham sedan going the other direction was closing fast. The car's massive shark nose grill could do a lot of damage too.

"Has she lost her mind?" Barnes yelled.

Meeker's eyes moved from the woman to the car and then beyond. In the shadows, a little girl no more than three was casually strolling out of an alley and onto the main street. Because of the morning sun's glare, it was doubtful the driver of the Graham could see the child. As Meeker held her breath, a galloping Worel dove forward, tackling the toddler rugby style before landing on her left shoulder and rolling back toward the alley. The car's driver, now aware that something was amiss, slammed on his brakes and slid to the right—coming so close to the woman his front bumper caught the heel of her pump, flipping the shoe from Worel's right foot and sending it flying into the air before it landed on the sidewalk in front of a hardware store.

"Did it hit her?" a shocked Bobbs asked.

"I don't think so," Barnes noted.

As Worel struggled to her feet, Meeker rushed across the street. By the time she arrived at the Brit's side, a dozen locals were studying the stranger holding the child in her arms. So much for trying to remain unnoticed and undercover!

"Who is she?" Worel softly demanded as she gently stroked the sobbing child's blonde hair.

The hardware store's owner stated what was quickly echoed by all the others at the scene, "We've never seen her before."

Meeker studied the child for a few seconds, looking into her clear green eyes, before turning her attention to Worel. "Are you okay?"

"I'm going to be sore tomorrow," the woman admitted, "and I might have to do some shoe shopping, but I'm fine."

Meeker nodded and then returned her attention to the child. Leaning close she whispered, "Who are you? What is your name?"

"Angela," came the soft reply.

"What's your last name?" Meeker asked.

"Brown. I'm Angela Brown and I'm three years old."

Meeker then noted a doll the child still held in her arms. "That's a beautiful doll you have."

"Her name is Audrey; my mother gave her to me."

"Where are you from?" Worel queried.

"Kansas."

"She's not in Kansas anymore," Bobbs wryly noted as she and Barnes joined Meeker.

"If her last name is Brown," Barnes chimed in, "then she might be tied into the woman Gertrude Root was looking for."

Meeker glanced toward The City Hotel and then looked back to Worel. "Gail, you may have just saved the clue to this whole mystery. Now, we just have to find out why her mother's not with her."

"Are you thinking what I'm thinking?" Bobbs asked.

Meeker nodded. "I've got to believe that Mrs. Brown is in a world of trouble. I think we need to find out." She took a deep breath before adding, "Let's hope I'm wrong."

CHAPTER 4

Monday, July 13, 1942
9:01 AM
Main Street, Taylorville, Illinois

Taylorville was like every other small American town. When something unusual happens, word spreads like wildfire. So naturally within minutes of Gail Worel saving the child, there were a few dozen citizens of all ages walking toward the hardware store from every direction. To protect their own identities and the reason they had swooped into town, Helen Meeker needed to hurriedly get things under control. She figured the best way to do that was provide a voice of assurance and act as though she was in charge.

"There's nothing to worry about here," she said to no one in particular but also to everyone within earshot. "This little child just wandered away from her mother who happens to be staying at the hotel. My sister, her husband, and I will go get the mom and bring her back to her child."

Bobbs frowned, leaned close and whispered, "My husband?"

"Just play along. I need to get rid of this growing crowd."

"Fine."

Meeker quietly announced to her team, "Gail will take care of Angela while the three of us find out how she snuck away from her mother." Turning back to toward the curious onlookers, she raised her voice and added, "Thank each of you for your help and concern, but as we know the family, we'll take it from here." She then looked toward Worel. "Gail, you take the girl over to the car. We'll go and find Mrs. Brown."

"I'll be happy to," the English woman quickly replied. "I wonder if Mrs. Brown knows she has a lovely daughter?"

As Meeker studied the still interested crowd to see if her ploy was going to work, the driver of the Graham, a short, balding man about sixty, handed Worel her shoe. After slipping it on, the Brit carried her charge back the car. As she did, the crowd began to break up and disperse. For the moment, things were working to the team's advantage.

As soon as Worel had Angela in the rented Ford, Meeker, with Bobbs and Barnes a step behind, marched to the hotel, entered through the double front doors and strolled over to the main desk. When no one walked up to greet her, Meeker spun the register around and studied the names. Peggy Brown had signed in last night at 10:14 and had been assigned Room 202. Meeker spun the register back into position and walked across the small lobby to the stairs. Fifteen steps up followed by a dozen more to her right placed her at her objective. Bobbs and Barnes had just arrived when their leader rapped on the door. There was no reply.

"Do you think she's in?" Barnes asked.

"Only one way to find out," Meeker suggested. "Becca, you got your tools?"

Pulling a purse from her shoulder, the blonde opened it and leaned close to the lock. She was just about to start picking it when Barnes reached down, twisted the knob and the door opened.

"Guess I should have tried that first," Meeker mumbled as pushed on the door and stepped in.

The room was a mess. The bed was unmade, a lamp was overturned and clothes were thrown everywhere. The disorder paled when compared to what was resting in the midst of it. On the floor at the foot of the bed was a woman. She was a fair-skinned redhead, dressed in a nightgown, slightly built and appeared to be about thirty. She was also very dead.

"Lead poisoning," Barnes grimly noted after closing the door and strolling to where the body lay.

"Likely all the shooter needed was one round," Bobbs added. "The bullet entered just above her right eye."

As Meeker stepped around the body and glanced into the connecting bath, Barnes observed, "Whoever killed her was looking for something. They tore everything up."

"As there are little girl's clothes everywhere," Bobbs tossed in. "I think we've found Angela's mother and this story doesn't have a happy ending."

Walking back into the room from the bath, Meeker's dark blue eyes locked onto something the other two had not yet seen. On the far side of bed was another woman. This one held a gun in her hands.

"The murder weapon was a thirty-eight," Meeker explained. "It was likely fired by a woman in her fifties."

Bobbs shook her head in amazement. "How do you know that?"

"Because I'm looking at her," came the response. "We've not only found Angela's mother, but we've found the general's wife."

As Meeker studied the limp form sprawled on the floor, Bobbs climbed over the disheveled bed and grabbed Gertrude Root's wrist. A few seconds later, she looked back to Meeker and noted, "Her pulse is strong. She might have been drugged or hit her head in the struggle. Doesn't appear to be anything serious."

Meeker frowned. This should have been simple. All they were supposed to do was track down a wandering wife and now they were dealing with a murder and what looked like robbery. Worst of all, for the time being they were going to have to cover it up.

"Well," Meeker groaned, "we can't go to the local cops, or we'll blow our cover and we can't just leave Root here for the police to find because that would create ramifications that would rock the Pentagon."

"Well," Bobbs cracked, "that certainly narrows our options. And what do we do about Angela?"

Meeker's eyes went to the dead woman who was apparently the child's mother. What was going to happen to the child? They couldn't take her with them, but they also couldn't turn her over to the cops. As she puzzled over that fly in the ointment, she looked toward her team. "Clay, you go get the car and bring it around to the rear of the hotel. Becca and I will figure a way to sneak Root out the back door."

"But what if she killed Peggy Brown?" Barnes demanded.

"We'll make sure she pays for it," Meeker assured him. "But for the time being, we have to protect her husband."

"What about the kid?" Bobbs asked.

"I saw a church about a block from the café," the team leader noted. "As we were waiting on Clay to scope out the hotel, I also saw a man with a clerical collar go into the building." Meeker made a quick decision that she hoped would be best for the child and their mission. "Clay before you pick us up, take Gail and Angela down to the church, give her to the pastor and explain the child is lost and we are from out of town and can't stay long enough to find her mother. Don't share the child's last name. We don't need the authorities discovering what happened in this room until we have Gertrude Root well clear of town. After you give Angela to the pastor, act as though you're headed out of town and then circle back here."

"Then where do we go?" Barnes asked.

"We'll head to Springfield and hole up," Meeker explained. "Once we find out what part Root played in this, we'll get her back to Washington and try to fit this puzzle together. Becca, you got your crime scene kit?"

"It's in the car."

"Good, I want paraffin tests on Root's hands even before she wakes up. I want to know if she shot this gun and killed this woman or if it was a frame. If it was the former, then we will have to find a way to make Root pay for the crime. If not, then it becomes our job to protect her and find out who was trying to set her up. Now, Clay, get going."

As Barnes exited the room, Bobbs, still kneeling over Root, asked, "How are we getting her out of here?"

"I noticed a laundry chute out in the hall," Meeker replied. "We're going to wrap her in a sheet and you and Mrs. Root are going to take a ride down to the basement. As maid service likely hasn't started yet, no should be down there now."

"And what if someone is there?"

"Then, Becca, you just explain you never outgrew your love of slides."

"Not a good plan," Bobbs noted as she pulled the gun from Root's right hand.

"Don't worry," Meeker announced, "I'll be in the laundry room waiting for you and I'll make sure no one else there."

"You wouldn't want to reverse roles would you?"

"Not today. Now help me get the sheet off this bed."

"Sure wish I'd have worn slacks," Bobbs growled. "Sliding down the chute in this dress is going not going to be very ladylike."

CHAPTER 5

Monday, July 13, 1942
11:15 PM
Springfield, Illinois

Helen Meeker opted to literally keep Gertrude Root in the dark. On the ride from Taylorville to Springfield, Root was blindfolded so even when she came out of her drug-induced coma, she could not see who was holding her. After checking into a motor court, the team continued to keep the woman from seeing the world around her. The blindfold didn't finally come off until Dizzy Vance arrived from Georgia. Because the private investigator was not officially undercover, he was the one who drew the assignment of grilling the general's wife. He kept after her for three hours before joining the rest of the team in a connecting cabin.

"What did you find out?" Meeker demanded as the middle-aged man dropped his heavy form onto a wooden desk chair.

"She claims she didn't shoot the woman and she doesn't even remember being in the room. It's days like this that make me yearn to drink again."

Clay Barnes pushed his lanky form against a far wall, loosened his tie and crossed his arms. "Did she have an answer on why she'd asked the clerk about Brown?"

"Yeah," Vance admitted while crossing one leg over the other and resting his elbows on his knees. "She claims this woman had some dirt on General Root and Brown had arranged the meeting to swap that dirt for some photos."

Meeker rose from her seat on the corner of the bed, walked over to a table, picked up a bottle of Coke and took a swig. After it had drained down her throat, she posed the obvious follow-up.

"What kind of dirt?"

"An affair," the investigator explained, "supposedly with an old flame from college."

"Enter a very well-made up Miss Rider," Barnes suggested. "Does that make her a suspect?"

"I don't see Constance getting her hands dirty," Meeker suggested, "but a enemy of the government might want those photos."

"Or," Barnes suggested, "an enemy of the administration. Jefferson Root and President Roosevelt are good friends so this might be a way to embarrass FDR."

"Who'd want to do that?" Vance asked.

"How about Hoover?" Meeker suggested.

"My goodness," Worel noted, "you Yanks have far more interesting lives than we Brits do."

A knock on the door caused every head to shift. When the first knock was followed by a second, Meeker looked toward Vance and nodded. He immediately got the cue and walked to the door. After cracking it and looking out into the night, he stepped back and Becca Bobbs entered. Only after Vance closed and locked the entry did the discussion continue.

"She didn't fire the gun," Bobbs noted. "The paraffin tests were negative. I also can assure you that someone fed her enough knockout drugs that it would have been easy to move her to the room and set her up for the frame. My guess is whoever set her up figured the room wouldn't be entered until about the time she was coming out of it."

"That makes sense," Meeker agreed. "What did you find via your calls to DC and Kansas?"

"Personally, I found out nothing," Bobbs admitted, "but your sister came up with some stuff. It seems Alison's sources are now much better than mine." She reached into her purse and pulled out a small pad. After glancing at the notes, she continued. "There have been some calls between the general's office and Miss Rider's home. Those calls have always been made late at night and have been going on for years."

"Fits," Vance cracked.

"And on Brown?" Meeker asked.

"Not much," Bobbs announced with a shrug. "She'd only lived in Overton, Kansas, for about a month. She didn't have any friends, she didn't go out, and her groceries were delivered. The landlady told Alison she knew Brown had a child, but the woman didn't take her out of the apartment so the

53

woman never saw her. There was no husband and she received no mail until the day she left. The landlady did remember the return address on that envelope was Cicero, Illinois. Oh, and the cops have discovered the body but in the four hours they've been working, they don't have any real leads."

"That likely means neither Root or us is tied to it," Meeker noted. "So, except for a tragic death and a now-orphaned little girl, it seems we have been given some good news. Or to put this another way, we've completed our assignment and gotten away clean. The President should be pleased."

"There is one complication," Bobbs announced. She paused before adding, "Because of Angela, the FBI has found a way to get involved. They stretched the case into a kidnapping and are searching for an English woman who looks a lot like Vivian Leigh as a material witness."

"Well, that's not cricket!" Worel exclaimed. "I saved a child's life and now am suspected of trying to nab her."

"It's a sticky wicket for us too," Meeker added, keeping with the British frame of reference, "we're working undercover while harboring a fugitive who's about to be the center of a nationwide manhunt."

"My mum won't like this," the Brit quipped, "and it does mess up the job I was brought here to do."

Meeker nodded. "Then, as long as we are killing time while we wait for our signal to do the Mexican job, let's solve this one. My days working with Henry at the FBI give me a bit of background in the type of work. As Dizzy is out completely of suspicion, just a private cop doing his own thing, he can go to Taylorville and scope things out." She glanced over to the investigator and smiled.

"Set the scene for me," Vance suggested. "I want to know the layout before I drive into this hornet's nest. Can someone draw me a map of the area where the murder was committed?"

"I can beat that," Bobbs chimed in. "While I was back at the plane doing my testing, I did our little English tourist a favor and developed her film. I have some very good eight by tens of the Main Street area."

The blonde opened a file and spilled a dozen prints out onto the bed. Worel was the first to make her way to the pictures.

"This is a great snap of you and Becca," the Brit announced picking up the top shot and handing it to Meeker. "Helen, your gray suit really photographs well. Wish I had that figure."

"Don't we all," Bobbs noted.

"It's not bad," Meeker agreed as she studied the photo. "We look pretty good for a couple of ghosts." She then moved over to the lamplight and studied the image more closely. While maintaining her focus, she posed a question. "Becca, do you have your magnifying glass?"

"You don't look *that* good," Bobbs quipped before reaching into her purse, withdrawing Sherlock Holmes's favorite tool and handing it across the bed. After taking it, Meeker turned back to her most trusted friend and partner.

"Has the time of death been fixed?"

"It was no earlier than a half an hour before we arrived on the scene," Bobbs suggested. "I only examined Brown briefly, but if I had to make a guess based on body temperature, then I'd say maybe even fifteen minutes."

"So we arrived soon after it happened," Meeker noted.

"Relatively speaking," Bobbs agreed.

"How long would you say," the team leader continued, "it was from the time we posed for these photos until we arrived at the room?"

Barnes chimed in, "It took me a couple of minutes to walk from the hotel to the car. I had just arrived when Gail became Wonder Woman."

"Who's Wonder Woman?" Worel asked.

"I'll buy you a comic book later," Meeker promised. "Okay, let's create the rest of the timeline. After Gail scooped up the little girl, we hung around the alley for about five more minutes. Then it took us another two or three minutes to walk to the hotel and maybe four more to get into the room."

"That's about right," Barnes agreed. "So if my math's correct, it was between ten and fifteen minutes."

Meeker took the photo and the glass over to the small table that supported the drab room's one luxury … a radio. Setting the radio to one side, she laid the photo down and leaned over to once again study the image … this time with the magnifying lens. A few seconds later, she smiled like the cat who'd just figure out the secret to opening a bird cage.

"Dizzy, look at this photo and tell me what you see."

The investigator pushed out of his chair and moseyed to the table. Taking the glass, he leaned over and studied every inch of the black and white image. Handing the glass to a curious Barnes so he could have his shot, Vance grimly smiled and nodded. Meeker was sure he now realized what had excited her.

"Clay," Meeker asked, "What do you see in the second-floor window of Brown's room?"

"There's a woman standing there looking out at the street," Barnes quickly noted.

"Who is it?"

"Gertrude Root."

As the other two women rushed to take their turn with the magnifying glass, Meeker shook her head and wryly noted, "Root was not drugged when this photo was taken and she was in that room. So she lied to us."

"But the paraffin tests came back negative," Bobbs argued.

"I didn't say she killed Brown," Meeker noted, "but she was in that room and mobile. And this would have likely been within minutes of when the woman was shot."

"She's not the only background player in this photo," Worel observed. There are three men visible. One is Clay, you can see him just stepping out of the hotel's front door, but there's another chap getting into an auto about twenty feet from the entrance and the third is leaning against a light post smoking a cigar."

"Let me take a loot at that," Barnes barked. Grabbing the glass, he studied the man on the right. "I don't know this guy." He moved the lens, paused and all but shouted, "But I'd swear the man getting into the car is the mystery man I saw with Fister in New Orleans."

"Wow," Meeker whispered, "how in the world does this tie into that mess?"

Barnes set the glass down and walked back to glance through the other photos. "Root's in a couple of more of these shots. And so are the other two. The man on the right is heading toward a light-colored Caddy and the man I recognized has gotten into a dark Oldsmobile and is driving off."

"Any license plates visible?" Meeker asked.

"No."

"So," Bobbs suggested, "I guess we need to have Dizzy grill Gertie some more."

"No," Meeker cut in. "Let's give her a clean bill and send her home. The President can have the Secret Service tail her. I think it's best if she believes we believe her story. Our surest bet now is to figure out who that other mystery man is and how and if he ties into the case."

Vance took a deep breath and hitched up his pants. "Losing too much weight," he noted. "And, just to prove my value to this group, we don't have to waste time digging up an ID. I know our mystery man. It is none other than the guy who took over Rudy Carfano's position … Jim 'Jaws' O'Toole."

"You're sure," the team leader demanded.

"I know Jaws pretty well, so you bet I'm sure."

"Dizzy," Meeker ordered, "Get back into that room, assure Gertrude Root we deeply appreciate her cooperation and we will make sure her name stays out of the news. Go so far as to even admit that we administered a paraffin test and it proved she was not involved. Then take her to the airport, buy her a ticket and get her headed back home."

"Got it."

"Becca, I want you to alert Alison that we need surveillance on Gertrude. Also, if possible, have the Secret Service tap her phone. Now, as her husband is a general, that might not be possible but if it is, I want it done. We need to know everyone who contacts her and what they have to say. As soon as she gets back to Washington, I want her observed around the clock. So have a team at the airport."

"I can do that."

"That's just the start," Meeker announced. "Tomorrow morning, I need you to go shopping. We're going to have to change Gail's look. I think using hair color would be better than a wig—maybe some glasses and some clothes that make her look frumpy."

"That's just ducky," Worel whined. "I come here as a halfway attractive member of the military only to be transformed into a cheap librarian."

Meeker ignored the complaining Brit and looked back to Vance. "Dizzy, I need you to go Taylorville early tomorrow. Do a little digging and see if anyone recognizes the men in those photos. O'Toole wasn't there as a tourist; he's bound to know someone in town. And try to find out what the FBI has uncovered. We need to know who their operatives are and what they're doing."

"And what do we do?" Barnes asked.

"After we give Gail a new look," Meeker explained, "we'll keep out of sight and wait for Dizzy to find enough information to set our next move."

CHAPTER 6

Tuesday, July 14, 1942
6:45 AM
Under the Atlantic Ocean near Florida

Henry Reese was soundly asleep in his bunk when the first explosion hit the U-boat. At first, he had no idea where he was. As he tried to shake awake, a second charge rattled the sub so badly that Reese rolled out of the bunk and onto floor. Bruised and still confused, he yanked himself upright. Rubbing the sleep from his eyes helped his mind to clear. Now he knew where he was and had a pretty good idea what had happened. Pulling on a shirt and pants, he sat down on his bunk to slip on his shoes as a third blast hit the underwater boat. This one was harder than the first two and, when the noise of the explosion subsided, Reese heard the sound of spewing water followed by a dozen different commands coming from all parts of the ship. A few seconds later, a voice screamed *Tauchen* over the intercom and the U-boat's nose dipped forward. The boat was heading deeper to try to avoid the enemy skimming along the surface of the ocean.

As the lights flickered on and off, Reese exited his quarters and slowly made his way down the corridor toward the heart of the ship. As he moved forward, German sailors rushed by him and the explosions continued. Each blast brought new rounds of leaks that were addressed by spinning knobs and men's curses. The scene playing out before him was chaotic and yet somehow organized. Even as the explosions continued and the ship rocked violently back and forth, there was no panic. No one had fallen to their knees in prayer or were begging to see their mother. So it was obvious this was not the crews' first dance.

The ship had leveled off by the time Reese reached the con. Leaning against a gray inside metal wall was Fritz Klein. With his arms crossed over his chest, it seemed the commander was watching disaster play out without any interest in its outcome. The short, thin man remained stoic even as his vessel pitched and rolled in the attack. Finally, after another round of blasts detonated even closer to the U-boat, Klein shrugged and gave the order to stop dead in the water. He then silently studied his men for a few moments. Only when all eyes were on him did the leader reveal his game plan.

"We'll play dead," he announced. "Gather up some clothes, cookware, a few books, and mix it in with oil and grease. After it's been launched through the tubes, then pass the word for everyone to remain in place and wait. It won't take long to find out if they swallowed the bait."

The men around him nodded and the word was quickly spread from station to station until the whole ship was alerted. Yet, even after the junk had been launched, the attack from the American ship didn't cease. For the next several minutes, the sub was rocked again and again.

"Men," the commander suggested, "we are in for a long day. We will just keep playing dead until they give up or we really are dead." After those around him nodded, Klein announced, "I'll wait in my cabin." Signaling for Reese to follow, the commander made his way back to his quarters. Once the two men were seated, the German leaned back in his bunk and stoically looked at the rounded ceiling. If he had any fear, he didn't reveal it.

"So much of life is a waiting game," Klein whispered. "We rush toward a battle and then we are forced to wait to see who wins. Or in this case, the battle has found us but still we wait to see if this is a loss or a draw."

"How long will they continue to attack?" Reese asked.

"You never know," came the quiet explanation. "It might be a few more minutes or until they run out of charges." He grinned. "And if one of those barrel bombs blows a hole in our hull, they might get to save the rest of their charges for another day. So we are either down here for a few hours or we are down here forever."

"Don't really like the sound of that," the American cracked in his best British accent.

"If the worst happens," Klein noted, "you'll be a lucky man. Those on a U-boat don't have to order a coffin; we're already in one. And like the ancient Egyptian royalty, you will be buried with a treasure. King Tut will have nothing on you, my friend.

That's not a bad legacy. Maybe someday someone will dig you off the ocean floor and make up the story of your life from what they found in the wreck."

Reese forced a smile. This was not the way he wanted to exit. When he died, he wanted his last breath to fill his lungs with fresh air.

"Fritz," the American noted, "you don't seem to fear death. I'm not sure I understand that."

"Well," the German grinned, "I don't welcome it, but I also recognize it is a regular visitor in war. We kill, they kill and people die by the millions. Why should it always be the other guy? What is it the Bible says, 'Those who live by the sword die by the sword.' That probably should be my epitaph."

"And," Reese cut in, "after this life ends, what's next?"

Klein returned his gaze to the ceiling as another charge hit to the starboard side. After the U-boat quit shaking, the commander put his hands behind his head and sighed. "Nigel, the Jew in me thinks that when my life ends it ends but, then again, I was not raised knowing much about my mother's people or their faith. So in the tug of war for my soul, I guess the Catholic part of might win out." He looked back at his guest. "You might have problems believing this, but I was an altar boy. No one was better or faster at lighting candles than I was."

"Another one of your many talents?"

He nodded.

"You didn't fully answer my question."

"There are times you avoid answering questions because you don't know the answers."

"So you have no guess?"

Klein shrugged, "There are other times when you don't answer because you don't want to admit what you believe. In this case, the Catholic in me wishes that life ends here. As many sins as I've committed, I'd hate to have to spend a few thousand years in purgatory paying for them."

The commander's fatalistic view didn't shock the visitor. In fact, he expected it. Reese had guessed the Sea Shark was a man who lived for the thrill found in the moment. In those brief times when he was in battle, he was likely very much alive and filled with a joy only those who thirsted for blood knew. But during the rest of the days, he was likely bored and brooding. He had enough depth of character he was likely also at war with his conscience.

The commander's solemn voice broke the silence, "How about you, Nigel? What's next for you?"

"Until I got into war," Reese admitted, "I was a firm believer in God and a pretty consistent follower of Christ. As I saw people die and as I killed people with my own hands, I began to wonder if there was a God and, if there was, why he didn't stop the senseless slaughter. So now I guess I'm a doubter who wants to believe rather than a believer who sometimes doubts."

Another charge rang out; this was well in front of the U-boat.

"They're moving away," Klein noted.

"So we fire up the engines and head in the opposite direction?"

"No, we play dead for a few more hours," the commander explained. "That ship has let others know about us and so a number of vessels will be hunting for our trail. Only when we detect no one above us will we try to come back to life."

"Try?" Reese asked with a raised eyebrow.

"We don't know the extent of the damage yet," Klein explained. "We may be hurt badly enough we can't rise. If that's case, then we are in for a slow death as our oxygen supply runs out."

The American shook his head. "You aren't helping my mood at all."

"Nigel, in moments like this, it's time to be honest. Con games are worthless when the stakes are this high." He glanced toward his guest, his expression now dead serious. "You're too noble to be a spy or be seduced by a trunk filled with treasure. On top of that, your accent comes and goes far too much for you to really be British. So who and what are you?"

His training kicking in, Reese didn't react to the accusations; instead he just grinned. "Maybe you're already suffering from a lack of oxygen. Your mind is delusional."

"Hardly," Klein shot back.

The visitor shrugged and fell back on a story he'd already invented for such an occasion. "Okay, my mother was American and I spent about six years there when I was a teen. Depending upon the level of stress, my accent does come and go."

"I'll accept that," the commander replied, "but our conversations still don't help me reconcile the other things I've noticed."

Reese joked, "What if I told you I'm a double agent and I'm not really selling the Allies out, I'm selling out Germany?"

Klein sat up in his bunk and studied his visitor's face in the dim light. After a few seconds, he reached across to the desk and opened the drawer. After shuffling through several documents, he retrieved the photo he shared earlier in the trip. He looked at it for a moment before handing it to Reese.

"What's this for?"

"If you are working for the Allies, then get this photo back to Washington. Let them know what's going on."

"Ah," Reese soberly replied, "and if I am who you think I am?"

"Then I'll not only be happy to help you get to your destination, but I'll have a new friend that I can respect rather than a passenger I could never understand." He quietly laughed before adding, "I guess your character will be defined by which you value you more … the payoff in treasure or that photo. If I'm any judge, it will be the latter. Now excuse me while I get back to my station."

Reese watched his host exit the cabin and make his way up the corridor toward the con. Once again alone, the American glanced back to the photo. The women in the picture were dead and yet they seemed to be crying out for justice. It was those cries that had been haunting Klein for months and now they were haunting Reese as well.

CHAPTER 7

Wednesday, July 15, 1942
9:01 AM
A farm outside of Springfield, Illinois

Fredrick Bauer stood on the stoop outside the back door of his farmhouse and studied the flat Illinois terrain. It was going to be a beautiful day, one made for sitting in the shade of an elm tree listening to a baseball game on the radio and drinking lemonade from a fruit jar, but he'd never done any of those things and wasn't going to do them today.

From the corner of his eye, he noted side door of the barn open. Stepping out into the sunshine was the man he'd made, broken, and thought he'd killed. Somehow Alistar Fister had lived through a half-dozen attempts on his life and a month of not getting the drug he needed to live. Yet that time of racing with the devil had taken a toll on the man's body while also humbling his self-esteem. Now even with his strength returning, the once huge ego had not returned, but perhaps this was still a man he could use.

"It's a wonderful day," the tall man announced as Fister approached.

"I guess," the younger man grumbled. "In truth, just knowing I'm going to live through it makes it good enough for me."

Bauer laughed. "It wasn't that long ago you thought you were king of the world. Now you're sounding like a pawn."

Fister frowned as he sat down on the steps. After folding his hands and resting his elbows on his knees, he wryly noted, "I've always been a pawn. I likely always will be."

Stepping down off the stoop and taking a place beside his charge, Bauer looked back toward a cornfield and made a suggestion that likely was not well received. "We each have our roles to play."

"And you're the puppet master."

The tall man shrugged. "Someone has to be and someone has to be a puppet. But I've given you many gifts and an incredible lifestyle. You've had more wine, women, and adventure in the past few years than most get in ninety."

"Except," Fister cracked, "I've always had to come back to you. There is no escaping that. Without the drug I'm …" He didn't finish his analogy.

"You're looking at this all wrong," Bauer explained. "I might be … let's call it … your boss, but you are superior to everyone you meet. That might not make you "the" god, but you are a god in human form. You used to relish that and you need to again. You need to embrace your power and use it."

Fister turned his head to look at the man pulling the strings and posed a question that needed no answer. "Do I have a choice?"

Bauer didn't reply, but instead rose, turned and walked back up the steps. When he got to the door, he casually said, "Follow me to my study."

After the stroll through the house to a room Fister knew well, it was time for the surprise. Strolling to the bookcase, Bauer carefully and quickly worked the combination of procedures needs to release a hidden latch. As he glanced over his shoulder, he noted his guest leafing through a recent issue of *Life* completely unaware of what had just happened. In the old days, Fister would have been watching his every move trying to find an opening or gain some kind of advantage. It was only when Bauer cleared his throat and made of show of revealing the hidden door and the stairs leading into a cellar that Fister dropped the publication and his jaw at the same time.

"What?"

Bauer pointed to box on his desk. "Open it."

Fister hurriedly took three steps to the desk, released the catch on the six by six-inch wooden container, and popped off the lid. Inside were scores of diamonds.

"There must be …"

"Hundreds," the host jumped in. "For Hitler, the fact the water we found creates madness is worth more than even if it had been the Fountain of Youth. That's the first installment on a delivery of the water I was able to secure in New Orleans before the Feds destroyed it. Yet, if we want more, we have to go to the source. I believe you know where that is."

71

Fister's face went blank. Dropping the diamonds he was holding in his hand back into the box, he shook his head. "I can't remember. In fact, there's a lot I can't remember."

The tall man nodded. "The fact the drugs I give you prevented the water from killing you doesn't mean it didn't affect your brain. You likely will have some memory issues. But we will retrace our steps to find that water. Hitler's not the only one who can use it. Now, pick up the box and follow me. We need to put the diamonds with some of the other bounty."

A confused Fister walked behind the Puppet Master through the now exposed entry and down a flight of stairs. As the dim light illuminated the large room, the visitor's eyes lit up in disbelief.

"My Lord," he whispered.

As Fister set the box on a table and began to scan the room's contents, Bauer grinned. "What you see before you are some of the finest, jewels, stashes of gold, and art in the world."

The guest nodded. "This place makes Tiffany's look like a junk store."

"If you had a real appreciation for art," Bauer suggested, "what glitters would not be nearly as important as what is framed."

As the shocked guest continued to survey the cache, his face suddenly went ashen white. Pointing his hand toward a dressed form in an ornate chair he whispered, "What's that?"

"Someone I used to love," came the simple explanation.

"But ..."

"Yes, she's a mummy and her once incomparable beauty has been transformed into a horrid representation of who she once was." Bauer moved toward the ghastly human monument.

As a stunned Fister watched, the tall man lightly traced the grotesque cadaver's cheek with his hand. "Love is a strange thing. Even when someone we love dies, the love doesn't. I love her as much now as I did twenty years ago. Of all the treasures in this room, she is the greatest."

"But why?" Fister whispered.

"A man who collects things has to share them with someone and I share them with her." Bauer turned his eyes from the form in the chair to his guest. "You are the only other man who has seen this room. Look around you and find something that will fit into your pocket."

Fister's gaze went from the woman back to the stacks of treasure. He quickly surveyed hundreds of items before visually latching onto a jade and diamond ring.

"Pick it up," Bauer suggested. "Slip it on. See how it feels." As Fister placed the huge gold ring on the index finger of his left hand, the tall man smiled. "You have good taste. That little item once belonged to Louis XIV. It was a gift from the Vatican. It was one of the first things Adolf shared with me after I did him a few favors."

Fister held his hand up and studied the ring in the light. "It's amazing."

"It's yours," Bauer shot back.

"But …"

The host waved his hand. "Don't say anything else. Now it's time to discuss business."

"So this ring is payment for a job I'm about to do?"

"Oh, no," Bauer assured him. "That is a down payment for past work. You'll get something far better if you complete this little matter."

After slipping the ring off his finger and dropping it into his shirt pocket, Fister crossed his arms and waited for his assignment. It didn't take long.

"The small town of Taylorville is your destination. It is an easy drive from here. The FBI is dealing with a little mess involving the murder of a woman in a hotel room. They have no suspects and the case would matter little if a child were not involved. The kidnapping of a three-year-old girl has made the little Illinois community a hotbed of activity."

"Doesn't sound like something you'd care about," Fister noted.

Bauer smiled, "I got word early this morning there is a woman being sent to record the facts in the case for J. Edger Hoover. She is the one I chose to replace you when you went rogue. Now that you're back, I think it's time to rid myself of her. Hence, I want you to prove yourself by rubbing her out."

Fister looked shocked, "You want to kill one of your own creations? I thought I was the only one who had that distinction."

"Let's just say I found a remarkable woman I thought could offer me certain skills you couldn't. But she is now out of control and knows far too much about me to live. Her name is Teresa Bryant. She is beautiful but deadly. You need to get rid of her without getting to know her. She has a seductive power that is unlike any woman I've ever encountered. So don't let her suck you in."

"And with all that going for her, you want her dead?"

"Yes, and even though it sounds easy, it's not. Like you, she has the drug in her blood. You can't just shoot her and walk away. You're going to have to go to the extreme."

Fister snickered, "It sounds as if you want her drawn and quartered."

The tall man's smile turned into a stoic frown. "If that's what it takes. And I want you to shoot a photo proving she's dead. I won't rest easy until I know she's no longer a problem."

"Okay," Fister replied, "but I wonder if you've thought about something else."

"What's that?"

"Now that I know about this room, what's to keep me from killing you and taking all this stuff for myself?"

Bauer smiled. "Without the shots, you'd die inside a month, so what good would all of this do you then? No, I'm not worried about you killing me, you need me too much."

CHAPTER 6

Wednesday, July 15, 1942
6:35 PM
Off the coast of Cuba

Henry Reese climbed the ladder up to the deck of the now surfaced U-boat and surveyed the ocean view. Taking in a deep breath of fresh air, he stretched and turned his attention to twenty crew members scrambling on top of the vessel and even diving into the sea. The ship had taken some damage from the depth charges. While it had been able to surface, it was going to need a bit of work before getting underway and the crew wouldn't sleep until that was accomplished.

"Sorry we won't be meeting our promised time schedule," Fritz Klein announced as he walked up to his guest. "If we can manage to stay undetected for a day or so, we can repair this old fish enough to get you to your rendezvous point, but we aren't going to make the speed we usually do."

Reese nodded, "I'm just grateful not to be visiting Davy Jones locker."

"In time, it's a place where most of us will take up residence," Klein casually replied. "At least that's true of seaman during a war. Let's walk forward."

As the two men approached the U-boat's nose, the commander glanced over his shoulder. He seemed to study his crew for a few moments before leaning close to Reese and whispering, "Do you have the photo?"

"It's in the cabin, hidden in my stuff. Do you want it back?"

"No," Klein assured him. "I want it to be shared." He paused, turned his face toward the sub's nose and nodded. "I guess I want to know if you're the man who will share it."

The American moved and faced the same direction as the German, put his hands behind his back and frowned. "You're assuming things you shouldn't. My name is Nigel Armstrong, I sold out my country and I'm taking my booty and spending my days living like a king."

"I don't care about the charade," Klein spat. "If you want to keep it up, that's fine with me."

Reese chuckled. "Doesn't the fact I haven't given you the name of the underground leader prove I don't trust Germans? In fact, I trust no one. Now do you want that photo back?"

The commander didn't immediately answer. Instead, he stared at the man towering over him as if trying to read his mind. When he finally did speak, he pushed the conversation in an entirely different and completely unexpected direction.

"I have a wife and two kids. My son is nine and my daughter, seven. My children think I'm pretty special. There's nothing I wouldn't do for them. Is there anyone in your life … that is … anyone you would die for?"

Reese nodded. "There was a woman and recently another who came into my life, but I don't know if I really love either of them or if it is just the time and the war that makes me think I do."

"That is another difference in us," Klein suggested. "I know I love my wife and treasure my children and that's the problem."

"How can that be a problem?"

"Because, those three lives stand in the way of my doing the right thing. They prevent me from sharing what I know." He paused and licked his lips. "Think about my logic if you will. Hundreds of thousands will be exterminated in camps over the next year … it might even be more … and those lives mean less to me than Gretchen, Bruno, and Sophie. I'm trading my love of my family for the destruction of my mother's people. What does that make me?"

"A husband and a father," Reese suggested.

"Maybe that's why priests don't get married," the commander grimly noted. "That way they can make decisions based on logic rather than out of love."

"So," the American asked, "if an Allied bomber dropped a load and wiped out your family, would you share what you know?"

Klein shook his head. "If that happened, I'd likely forget what I know and seek revenge on those who wiped out my reason for living."

"Unlike you," Reese noted, "I'm aware of who the enemy is. You don't know. On one hand, it is Hitler and on the other, it is the Allies. I'd think it would be hard to fight a war if you were constantly debating within yourself which side was morally right and which was wrong."

The commander turned to face his guest. "Who is the enemy?"

Reese took in deep breath of salt air as he pondered the question. When he finally gave his reply, it was cryptic and buried in logic usually reserved for a philosophy or theology class. "The enemy is your inability to decide what is most important. Any good commander knows the needs of the many outweigh the needs of the few."

"So I should sacrifice my family?"

"You do the math," the American suggested. "I'm going back to my quarters and wait."

CHAPTER 9

Friday, July 17, 1942
8:35 AM
Taylorville, Illinois

Dizzy Vance, dressed like a farmer in bib overalls and a worn and stained blue and red St. Louis Cardinal's baseball hat, had been tailing the man and a woman for eighteen hours. During that time, the pair had seemingly found nothing pointing to who was behind the murder of Peggy Brown. When the pair stepped into the café to grab breakfast, Vance found a pay phone and checked in with the team.

"There's no reason to come up yet," the investigator suggested.

Meeker's reply was immediately, "Well, we're not doing any good here, so we'll come to Taylorville anyway. We'll take a couple of rooms at the hotel."

"Is that wise?" Vance asked.

"It's the safest place in town," she assured him, "and it might give us a chance to take another look at the crime scene."

"But what about the Brit?" the investigator asked.

"She looks more like Joan Blondell than Vivian Leigh now, so she'll be fine. The rest of us have made a few physical changes as well. Bobbs is wearing a red wig, mine is blonde, and some good make-up and a gray hairpiece has aged Clay about thirty years. So, anything else you need to report before we sneak into town?"

"Yeah, I'm not the only one watching the FBI team. There's another guy who's shadowing them too. He's a good-looking dude who seems to be waiting for something to happen. I have no idea what. I'm in a phone booth across from the café and he's fifty yards down the street sitting on a bench."

"Has he spotted you?"

"I don't think so, his focus on strictly on the G-men … or G-woman anyway. And since when did Hoover put women in the field?"

"She's likely there to take notes, type them up and file them for the lead investigator."

"Figures. I'll see you later."

Vance hung up the phone and stepped into the hardware store. While keeping his eyes glued to the café, he shifted through various sized bolts and nuts. Staying in his cover, he bought a handful of the fasteners and stuffed the paper sack into his pocket. He was just stepping back into the sunshine when the FBI agents exited the eatery. They paused outside, talked for a few seconds and then headed in different directions.

The investigator was at loss. Who should he follow? Logic told him the man was the one in charge and he was about to follow him when he noticed the other tail. The mystery man was following the woman. Why? Perhaps that was the most important question that needed to be answered. Playing a hunch, he turned and tailed what he could only describe as one good looking dame wearing a skirt so tight it seemed painted to her hips. As he admired the woman's walk, he wondered how she'd managed to get the skirt on.

Moving his eyes from the female to the man in the picture, Vance waited for the shadow to walk by his position before turning right and trailing him and the G-woman. This was an interesting game of cat and mouse. Did that make him the dog?

Casually crossing the street, the investigator kept one eye on the man and the other on the woman. She was now just about twenty-five yards ahead. As neither was moving quickly, it gave him the time to stop and take stock of both.

The woman was likely in her early thirties. She was built like a Hollywood bathing beauty. Outfitted in a light gray suit complete with the already noticed form-fitting skirt, she also wore a white blouse and pumps and carried a purse the size of a duffle bag. Her stride was long and straight with her dark hair bouncing at her shoulders with each step. And though she was not moving quickly, as she neither looked right nor left, she appeared to be on a mission.

The man was dressed casually in dark slacks, tan sports coat, and a light blue shirt. His eyes were clear and he moved with a casual but athletic gait. His hair was slightly wavy and cut in a

Gary Cooper style. He hadn't bothered with a hat. He could have been just like any other young man in town shopping except for one thing ... the way the jacket hung indicated he was wearing a shoulder holster. That was not the norm in Taylorville.

Vance had just begun to step forward when the woman passed a small grocery store and made a left into an alley. The investigator paused and acted as though he was studying a display in a drugstore window when, in fact, he was observing the man across the street. After glancing both directions, that man jogged across the street and also rushed into the alley. Something was up!

Reaching into his pocket, Vance felt for his gun. Satisfied he would be able to easily retrieve it from the overalls' oversized pocket, he picked up his pace. Thirty steps later he was at the alley. Taking a deep breath, he peered around the corner. Seventy-five feet to his left the man had the woman cornered. His weapon was no longer concealed; it was drawn and ready for action.

There were few options open. The investigator could stay out of sight and let things play out or he could make a break a get involved. Neither one of those choices was very appealing. Either way he was going to be a large, easy to hit target. He was about to force his overweight body into an Olympic-style sprint when he noted a door opening from the grocery store out into the alley. Reversing course, he entered the business, moved quickly over to the far aisle and toward the rear of the store. There was a meat counter at the back of the building where a white-clad butcher was engaged in a conversation with an elderly woman. They seemed to be arguing about the cost of baloney. Their conversation was so heated, neither saw Vance push open a door leading to a storeroom. Now, just fifteen feet ahead was the windowless exit that would give him access to the alley. Breathing heavily, he covered the distance in seven steps, leaned in and slowly twisted the knob with his left hand. With his gun ready in his right, he eased the door open about an inch. Through the crack he could see the woman and, based on the shadow beside her, Vance knew the man was directly beside the door. If his math was right, ramming the door open would send the man sprawling. But first he wanted to see if he could hear a bit of the conversation.

"Why me?" the woman asked. "Were you involved in the woman's murder?"

"I've never been to this town before," came the quick reply.

"Then why are you here?" she demanded.

"To complete a job," he explained. "Our boss wants you out of the way."

Through the crack in the door, the investigator observed the woman smile and then quip, "You're Fister. Everyone thought you were dead."

"As you can see I'm not."

"And with you back, I'm not needed. At least that is what he thinks. Taking me here is a mistake. Someone will hear and then you'll be spotted. You don't have a chance to make it out alive."

"The gun has a silencer," he explained, "we're alone; it will be awhile before anyone finds your body and I'll be long gone by then."

"Back to the farm," she jabbed.

"Where else? Now say your prayers."

There was no reason to wait any longer. Putting his shoulder into the door, Vance shoved it open, knocking the surprised man he now knew as Fister to his knees. As the stunned victim tried to focus on a new target, the investigator kicked out with his right shoe catching the fallen Fister in the left eye, the blow opening up a two-inch long cut that immediately gushed blood. Not waiting to admire his footwork, Vance took a step forward and brought his revolver down hard on Fister's head. That blow caused the would-be killer to waver for a moment before he fell from his knees face first onto the dusty pavement.

The woman was no longer a victim or a spectator. Moving quickly forward, she yanked the gun from Fister's hand and delivered another blow to the side of his head with her pump. Only then did she step back to study her savior.

"Thanks."

"No problem," Vance announced as he shoved his own weapon back into his pocket.

"Not many farmers carry handguns," she noted.

"I only have this one," the investigator lied, "because it's been over at the hardware store being fixed. I'm glad I didn't have to use it." He modestly shrugged as he continued his lie, "I've only shot it a couple of times and I can't really hit anything." As he finished his explanation, he wondered if she bought it. When he was unable to read her expression, he added, "Guess we better get the cops over here so they can arrest this man."

"That won't be necessary," she assured him. "My name's Bryant, I'm with the FBI and we're working a case here. I think this guy might be involved." She paused, reached into the purse and retrieved a pair of handcuffs. "Would you mind putting these on him?"

"Not at all," Vance answered. Grabbing the cuffs, he yanked Fister's arms behind his back and locked the bracelets into place.

"Thanks," the woman almost sang out. "Now why don't you go on about your business?" The question was a delivered like an order.

"Are you sure you don't want me to stick around," the investigator asked.

"No, I've got things under control now. When this guy comes to, I'll march him back to my partner. And if you'll give me your name and address, I'm sure Mr. Hoover would want to express his thanks for your service."

"J. Edgar?" he said, as if impressed.

"One and the same."

"That's okay," Vance announced, "I'm kind of shy about attention and my wife would be really upset if she thought I'd put my life on the line. So your thanks are enough."

The last thing the investigator wanted to do was leave, there were too many questions that had not been asked much less answered, but there was no real excuse for staying. Turning, he walked down the alley toward the street pondering just who the man he'd knocked out was and how he and Bryant worked for the same man. That bit of knowledge had to mean something, but what?

CHAPTER 10

Friday, July 17, 1942
9:35 AM
Taylorville, Illinois

As soon as the farmer who'd stepped into the role of unexpected savior disappeared around the corner, Teresa Bryant rolled a battered Alistar Fister over and dragged him by his collar along the alley before depositing the man on the far side of a half dozen smelly trash cans. It was obvious from the odor someone had tossed away spoiled fish. As she studied the still unconscious man, Bryant seemed to think the ghastly, stomach-churning aroma was the perfect environment for dealing with scum like Fister. Pushing his still limp body against the brick wall and propping him into a sitting position, she took a lid from the nearest can, chased off a surprised rat, frowned and dug through a layer of old produce until she found an empty tin can. Noting a spigot on the back wall of the grocery, she walked the twenty feet to it, turned it on and filled the can. She retraced her steps, hovered over the unconscious man and tossed the water into his face. After throwing the can to the side, she lightly slapped Fister's cheeks a few times until his eyes fluttered.

"Wake up," she demanded with something other than a charming bedside manner. "Snap out of it, you bumbling fool!"

He shook his head, eyes rolling around like marbles for a few seconds before they finally began to focus. As he realized who was now standing over him, Fister instinctively tried to reach out with his hands only to discover his arms locked in place by the handcuffs. Resigned to his fate, he slumped back against the dirty brick wall.

"You failed," Bryant smugly announced. "I hold your fate in my hands. Now before we decide how this little drama concludes, we have a few things to get straight."

"Just get it over with," he groaned. "To add to the irony, why don't you use my gun?"

"I'm not letting you off that easy," she shot back. "As I see it, I have three options and I'll let you make the call on which one I use." She pushed his head back against the wall with her high heel pump and smiled. "Don't get any ideas. If I have to, I'll shoot you and not lose a moment of sleep over your passing." Releasing her foot, she moved two steps to the man's right and posed a question.

"Why did Bauer want me dead?"

Fister licked a bit of blood from the corner of his mouth before announcing, "You're out of control."

"No," she argued, "I'm completely controlled and that's what drives him crazy." She chuckled, "So you were his prize experiment. You were the man he bragged about being superhuman. My goodness, you allowed a fat old farmer to take you out with one kick to the face." She leaned closer, "And your eye doesn't look very good. I think there will be a scar."

"I'm a bit off my game," Fister cracked.

"If I make the call," she snapped, "the game's over. Anyway, let's get back to what just happened when the hayseed took you out. As I understand it from our conversation, you were supposed to kill me. If you had actually accomplished that, what were you to bring back as proof that I was dead?"

"A picture; there's a camera in my pocket."

"Makes sense," she said with a nod, "it would be hard to explain if someone saw you carrying my dead body down the street. But we don't have to worry about my posing for a picture now. So, with the murder option out, what do I do with you?"

"Don't tease me," he begged, "just kill me. I've been more dead than alive for weeks."

"That's not really very productive for either one of us," Bryant noted. "So the next option would be turning you over to the FBI. Of course, they'll be shocked you're alive but I can explain you had a twin and you somehow passed his dead body off as yours. As I think about it, considering you're working with Bauer, I can likely pin Killpatrick's murder on you too."

"You won't have to pin it," Fister suggested, "I'll confess. I did it. That guy was a jerk."

At least Fister was right on that count. Bryant's gaze went to one of the trashcans. Another rat was pushing its head out from under a spoiled potato to take in the show. She wondered if the rodent sympathized with her captive. After all, they did have a lot in common.

"You know," Bryant declared with a hint of pride, "if I brought you in and gave you to Hoover, I might look heroic. Yet, if I did that, you'd tell what you know about Bauer and I'd hate seeing everything he's done fall into J. Edgar's hands. I think he'd misuse it. So that brings us to option three."

"I don't see an option three," he cracked. "You either kill me or give me to the FBI? What else is there?"

The beautiful woman walked back to where she once again hovered over Fister. Smiling, she bent over until they were nose to nose. Tracing the wound on his cheekbone with the barrel of the gun, she whispered, "The other option is working with me."

He shook his head. "That's a short-term employment opportunity. In a few weeks, I'd need the stuff. When I didn't get it, the seizures would start and things would go downhill from there. I'd rather die right now with a shot from that gun than waste away with my body gripped by uncontrollable fits."

She pulled the pistol back and nodded. "Yeah, I can see how that wouldn't be appealing, but what if I told you I can supply you with the injections?"

A look of disbelief crossed Fister's face. "He's the only one who has the stuff."

"He was the only one," she explained as she moved away from the man. "Among other things, I'm a trained chemist. I stole the stuff, used the FBI lab and have created a large supply of his miracle snake oil. I can create more anytime I want to. So working with me is anything but a death sentence."

"But ..."

"Stand up," she barked.

Pushing his shoulders against the wall, Fister bent his knees and used his feet to slide his back along the dirty bricks. Once he was standing, Bryant glanced both ways, put the gun into her purse and posed her next question.

"What do you know about Bauer?"

The man shrugged. "He has an agenda, he doesn't take sides, though, ironically, everyone thinks they are on his side. Oh, and he has a plan for after the war to become a very powerful and wealthy man."

"What about his background?"

"I don't know much about that," Fister explained, "other than he must have really loved someone once. After all, he still keeps her body."

"What?"

"He has a mummy in a storeroom at his home," he explained. "It's dressed up in antique clothing and sitting on a chair. He told me he still loves her."

Bryant turned her eyes from Fister to the wall. Finally, a glimpse into the tall man's past! But what does it mean?

"You don't know anything else about the woman?" she demanded.

"I didn't even see her until yesterday. He took me to a hidden room and she was there along with a lot of other stuff."

"Stuff?"

"Yeah, valuable stuff … gold, diamonds, paintings, and more. It's all payoffs from the Nazis for favors Bauer's done for them."

This was more information than she could have hoped for. But could she use it to her advantage and in the process not tip her hand?

"Turn around," she barked. After the man complied, she inserted the key into one side of the cuffs and freed his left hand from the restraint. She then stepped back. When Fister turned to face her, she tossed him the key and silently watched him unlock the other side. "Okay, give the cuffs to me. I don't need to lose them; my partner and J. Edgar wouldn't like that." After he'd complied and she'd stored the items in her bag, she pulled the clip from the gun and emptied the bullets into her purse. She then tossed it back to its owner.

"What next?" he asked.

Reaching back into her bag, she retrieved a small bottle filled with clear liquid. She studied it for a moment before tossing that to him as well.

"That's enough for two doses," she explained. "I have a lot more, but this will prove my value to you."

He looked at the gift and then back to her. "So I just take your word that this is the real deal."

"You take his word," she shot back, "and he's the one that keeps a dead woman as a memento from the past."

94

Fister frowned. "You're not letting me live just because you are a charitable soul."

"No. I'm giving it to you because I can use you." She pulled a card from her pocket and shoved it his way. After he took it, she continued, "That gives you a way to get in touch with me. So if you need more stuff, I can get it to you."

"Yeah, but there's always a catch to a gift, especially when that gift is the gift of life."

"Of course, there is," Bryant noted. "I want you to find out who that dead woman was. I also need to know as much about Bauer's past as possible. That means I have to have his contacts here and in Germany. Also, if he's planning something big, I want to know what, when, and where."

"You're not asking much," Fister grumbled. "I mean when I go back without your scalp, he might just do me in."

"You just explain to him that by the time you got here, I was already in Chicago."

"And what makes you think he'll believe it?"

"Follow me," she suggested.

Though she was convinced she had Fister where she wanted him, Bryant still kept her hand on the gun in her bag. If he made one move toward her, she'd have no qualms about taking him down even if that made getting the information she needed a bit harder. He must have sensed her resolve because not once during their two-block walk down the back alley did he make one misstep. After leading him into a back door and down a hall at the Taylorville Inn, the city's only other hotel, she retrieved a key and pushed open the door to 109. Once inside she pointed to a chair beside the bed. He didn't argue.

"What now?"

"You just wait and see."

After pulling her gun out and setting it on a table beside the phone, she rang the front desk, informed them she was making a call that should be billed to her room and asked for the long distance operator. When the voice came on the line, she gave the woman a number. As the operator was dialling, Bryant covered the mouthpiece and glanced back to her guest. "Do you recognize that number?"

"It's the farm," he replied.

"Hello."

"This is Bryant, I'm in Chicago. Is there anything I can do for you while I'm here?"

"I was told you were with the FBI team in Taylorville."

"I was, but a lead sent the man I'm with North. Didn't figure you'd need anything in a Taylorville, but Chicago might be a different story."

"No, I'm fine. Contact me when you get back to DC."

Bryant didn't bother with a goodbye before hanging up.

"Now, Mr. Fister, you have a excuse for not getting me this time."

"How do I explain my face?" he asked.

"You can come up with a story," she assured him. "I suggest you drive your car into a fence post on the way home. Now do we have a deal?"

"I have to know the stuff's good," Fister answered.

"That's fair," Bryant admitted. "When you're convinced, call me. Now get out of here."

He stood and turned toward the door. After taking three steps, he looked back to the woman. "I don't get the percentages. Why should I join you? What have you got to offer than I don't already have?"

"Freedom," she explained. "That's what you thought the water would get you."

"How did you know about that?" he demanded.

"I've been to the farm too and when I was there, I learned all about you. Now you get moving and start to think about what it would be like to have a half share of all that Bauer has and have your freedom too."

Fister moved to the door, opened it and disappeared. Walking over and closing the entry, Bryant smiled. The Puppet Master was about to be her puppet and he would never know about the strings she'd be pulling.

CHAPTER II

Saturday, July 18, 1942
8:35 AM
Taylorville, Illinois

Meeker, wearing a matronly country dress, flats, a wig and no make-up was waiting alone for Vance at the café. After the investigator arrived, he took a place with the woman at a table in front of the window looking out on Main Street. After ordering something called the Double-Hitter Breakfast, he filled her in on the events of the day before. Once he finished sketching an overview of his work, Meeker dug for details.

"So you saved the woman working with the agent?"

"Yeah," he admitted while taking a sip of black coffee. "I got lucky on the location of a door. But the strange thing was something she told the wannabe shooter before I stepped in."

After taking a sip of tomato juice, Meeker nodded. "What was that and does it have anything to do with either O'Toole or the man we're trying to identify that Barnes spotted when he was in New Orleans?"

"No, I drew blanks on that," the investigator admitted, "but the guy did say something that made no sense. He told her they worked for the same man and, it seemed if I heard things right, that guy wanted her dead."

"She works for Hoover at the FBI," Meeker noted. "Why would he want her dead? From what we've found out, she was the key in getting back the girl that was kidnapped in Tulsa."

"I know things don't line up," Vance admitted. "Yet nothing about that guy spelled out FBI agent. They all seem to have a look." He paused and smiled, "In fact, I think they all walk alike too. I wonder if they teach that as a part of their training? Anyway, this guy didn't look or walk like a G-man."

"When we get back to Drury, we'll do some more digging on the woman's background," Meeker suggested, "Right now, we need to figure out who killed Peggy Brown and why. Has the FBI come up with anything the locals missed?"

Vance picked up a spoon and dipped it into his coffee. After stirring it a bit, he looked back at the woman. "To my knowledge, they know nothing but from what I've observed they've pretty much left no stone unturned."

"I worked with them enough to admire their methods," Meeker admitted. "What about this guy you knocked out and handed over to them. Could he have been the killer?"

The investigator shrugged. "She never accused him of it. My gut tells me that Fixter's only job was to bump her off."

"What did you say his name was?" Meeker asked.

"Fixter is what it sounded like to me."

"How about Fister?"

"Yeah, maybe that was it. Why?"

"So Reggie's not dead?" she whispered. "After all this time, I thought he must have joined his brother."

"Reggie?"

Her tone now much more intense, Meeker leaned close to Vance and posed a question. "What do you know about me?"

"I've read the file they gave me before I joined your little band. I know about your time with the FBI. I know the leaders of the free world pretty much owe you their lives."

"Then you know that someone tried to kill me."

"Yeah … wait," the investigator looked down into his coffee cup and shook his head. "I remember now the guy who tried to gun you down was Fister." He paused, looked back at the woman and, in an apologetic tone, asked, "Did I give that guy to the FBI."

"No," Meeker assured him, "that Fister is dead, but his twin brother, who used to work for us, is missing."

"So why," the man inquired, "would he want to take out the woman?"

"And how would they have the same employer?" Meeker whispered. "The man you handed over was once on our team. She's not."

"Has he turned?" Vance wondered.

"Was he ever really on our side?" The woman's observation was delivered with an arched eyebrow.

Meeker turned her eyes to the front door. Having just entered, Becca Bobbs, also dressed conservatively and wearing a wig, was surveying the room. When she spotted Vance and Meeker, she quickly made her way to the table. After Bobbs was seated, Meeker asked, "You got something?"

"A bit of background on Gertrude Root we didn't have before. It seems she often goes on visits to her sister in Chicago."

"What's unusual about that?" Vance asked.

"She has no sister," Bobbs explained.

"Has she been having an affair?" the investigator quipped. "I would have never thought that was possible."

"Who knows?" the blonde answered. "There has never been a reason to follow her until now. But I can add this little tidbit that you'll find intriguing. Root got on the plane in Springfield, but she didn't ever make it to Washington. Somewhere she got off and disappeared. She did call the general, told him she was fine and going to spend a few days with …"

"Let me guess," Meeker cracked, "her sister in Chicago."

"You got it."

"That puts Gertie back on the suspect's list," Vance suggested.

"Well," Bobbs added, "there is a bit more that Alison was able to dig up using White House contacts. The woman who was murdered has an interesting background as well. Her maiden name was O'Toole and she does have a sibling in the Windy City."

"Jaws is her brother?" the investigator asked.

"Yep," Bobbs assured him, "so now we have a reason for him to be Taylorville."

"But why here?" Meeker asked. "Why not Chicago?"

The blonde smiled, "The reason for not meeting in the big city is pretty simple. No one in the organization knew about her. Jaws has erased a lot of his past—likely to protect those friends and family members not in his gang. But thankfully, there are census reports and records at Ellis Island."

"That makes sense," Vance added, "He'd naturally want to protect her. But I think there is another reason too. If you're embedded into a community, go to church, teach school, and have a family, no one looks at you. Thus, when a special delivery is needed, those folks can do it without anyone actually noticing. You don't use them very often, but you always have them in reserve. The same can be true for a mother with a small child. There are times when someone like that is much more useful to a criminal organization than those with a record. Add to the fact Jaws could no doubt trust her much more than he could anyone else."

"Okay," Meeker noted, "I get the reason for him not meeting with his sister in Chicago or even where she lived in Kansas, but why Taylorville?"

"Because," Bobbs explained, "The City Hotel is owned by a company that can be traced back to the late Rudy Carfano. And what makes this even better is the manager of the business has now disappeared. The FBI has him as the primary suspect and he's slipped completely from sight. In fact, the Bureau has been watching him for at least six months. Coming up here to work this case might have been an excuse to track him down."

"What's his name?" Vance asked.

"John Smith," she quipped, "and he had only been the manager for six days. I have no idea what his real name is. According to the records Alison found, he has about a dozen."

As she tried to put the pieces of the puzzle together, Meeker drummed her fingers on the table. Brown was here to meet her brother. Someone in the organization who had a vendetta against Jaws O'Toole, likely a person loyal to Carfano and figuring that O'Toole was behind the hit on Carfano, found out about the meeting and put a man in place to knock her off as an act of retribution. That's the only thing that made sense. She looked over to Bobbs.

"Does the FBI know about Brown's connection to O'Toole or that the mobster was in town on the day she died?"

"Not yet, but it's just a matter of time. You know they will figure it out at some point. They are pretty good at connecting the dots if there are enough of them."

"Then," Meeker suggested, "that means they'll see Smith as the only suspect."

"Isn't he?" Vance asked.

"No," the team leader answered. "Maybe he pulled the trigger and maybe he didn't, but what we know that the FBI doesn't know is that Gertrude Root was in that room and photos prove she was very much conscious and aware about the time Brown was killed. A hit man doesn't frame anyone; he just does his job and walks away. So Smith wouldn't have framed her. So what part does Root have in this?"

Bobbs nodded, "Maybe she was in the wrong place at the

wrong time. Maybe she was meeting someone here … the person who she claimed was her sister."

"No," Meeker argued, "there was no reason for her to be in Brown's room unless she had business there." She looked back to Vance and then the woman to her right. "And there is something else that Dizzy told me that turns this whole thing upside down."

"What?" Bobbs asked.

"Reggie Fister was in town trying to knock off the woman working for the FBI. Dizzy stopped Fister and turned him over to the woman. So now they have the guy who we thought worked for us and he can blow our cover in a split second. Let's face it, Fister has the power to unwrite our obituaries."

Bobbs shook her head. "I can assure you of this. The FBI doesn't have anyone. So the woman never turned Reggie or anyone else over to them."

"Why not?" a confused Vance demanded.

Meeker frowned. Nothing was as it appeared. Everything was upside down.

"Okay, forget about everything else for the moment. Let's turn our attention to perhaps the most important element in this case. Let's find the woman working with the FBI and tail her. At this moment, keeping her quiet is the key to keeping our organization working."

"What about Root and the Brown murder?" Vance asked.

"Minor league stuff," Meeker suggested looking at the café's baseball themed decorations, "and we're playing in the majors right now. Dizzy, you're still undercover. Find that woman and

105

keep an eye on her. Becca and I'll go back and share what we know with Clay. Then we'll wait to hear from you and plan our next move based on ..." Meeker turned to Bobbs, "Do we know her name?"

"The FBI woman's?" Bobbs asked.

"Yeah."

"Teresa Bryant; she's a secretary in Hoover's office."

"Let's see what we can dig up on Miss Teresa Bryant."

CHAPTER 12

Saturday, July 18, 1942
9:35 AM
Taylorville, Illinois

Teresa Bryant, dressed in a baby blue shirt and yellow blouse, observed Chet Morris search the dead woman's hotel room for the tenth time. Just like the first nine, he again came up empty.

"Nothing to tie anyone to this crime," he barked in angry. "It's simply perfect. A mother checks into a room, she knows no one in town, she has no reason to be here, she gets no calls and only leaves the room on three occasions. The first is to go the hardware store down the street where she buys a bag. The second is when she went to the café to pick up breakfast to go. On the final occasion, she walked to the front desk to drop off a suit to be cleaned and pressed and then she took a short stroll around town. Supposedly no one visited her. Did I point out that she received no calls?"

Bryant nodded and walked over to the window looking out on Main Street. It was Saturday morning and the farm families were pouring into town to shop. Cars and trucks occupied all the parking spaces, women filled the grocery store, men were filing in and out of the hardware store, and children were racing toward the Five and Dime. And perhaps out there with them was a murderer. But where do you start looking for a needle in this rural haystack?

"What could we have missed?" Morris called out.

As she turned, the woman's fingernails lightly scraped the windowsill. Glancing down, she noted ashes. Pinching a bit of them between her finger and index finger, she brought them up to her nose.

"Chet," she asked, "no one's smoked in here have they?"

"I don't think so," he assured her. "The local cop who investigated the room didn't smoke; I know because I asked him for a light. And he locked the room when he left. No one entered until our Chicago team arrived to process the scene and they know not to smoke. Why?"

"Because there are cigar ashes on the windowsill. The maid told us she thoroughly cleaned and dusted the room before Brown moved in and I doubt if the dead woman smoked a stogie. She didn't seem the type."

"So," Morris mused as he walked over to the sill, "she had a visitor."

"A man," Bryant added, "who smoked cigars." She again studied the room, not so much looking to see what was here but what wasn't. As she continued her inventory of the missing, she asked, "What did the boys find in her car?"

"The usual," he announced, "road maps, some cosmetics, a few kid's toys, and some loose change."

"And nothing in her handbag or the suitcase that was out of the ordinary?"

"No."

Bryant looked at the dead woman's purse and then toward the two suitcases that were sitting on the bed. "Where's the other bag?"

"What bag?" he asked.

"The one she bought when she went shopping? The two on the bed are worn, so it's not one of them."

Morris's eyes went to the bed and then back to Bryant. "What are you thinking?"

"The woman needed another bag, so she made a special trip out to get one. No one saw her daughter on that trip or the other two she made. A good mother wouldn't have left kid alone all three times and she wouldn't have bought a bag she didn't need. The stuff she brought with her doesn't even fill the two suitcases she owns, so why get another one and where is it now?"

"So that's the key?" Morris asked.

"You have to think like a woman," she explained. "There are several keys. She checked in late and according to the night clerk, she brought her own bags to the room. He did see a blonde girl walk through from the car, but then he told you he went back to the office to listen to the radio. So a man could have come in after she checked in and gotten to her room with no one seeing him. That man must have stayed in the room when Peggy Brown went out. He took care of the kid and must have smoked a cigar to pass the time."

"So," the FBI agent noted, "He was likely her husband, brother, or friend."

Bryant waved her finger. "It doesn't have to line up that neatly. He could have been holding her for something she had. The kid would have been left behind when she was running errands to make sure she didn't go to the cops."

Morris shook his head. "That sounds far-fetched to me."

"We have no idea who the man is … either friend or foe, so, using a woman's logic, I believe the thing we need to find is the bag."

"The killer must have taken it," the man suggested. "So we aren't going to have a prayer of finding it. No fingerprints, no murder weapon, no suspects, and no witnesses; that makes this the perfect crime."

Bryant crossed her arms and studied the room. Every corner had been searched, the drawers pulled out of the chests, the mattress turned over and anything that had been hanging on the wall had been taken off. Morris had even pulled the top off the commode and searched the tank. There were no hidden compartments in the purse or the bags and nothing had been stashed away in the pockets of the clothes. The only keys on the women's key ring were to the car and a room where Brown had lived for a month in Kansas. The man was right, there were no solid clues. Then it hit her. Maybe she was thinking like a woman when she needed to be thinking like a mother.

"The kid, where is she?"

"She's with the babysitter we hired," Morris said with the shrug, "they're in a room down the hall. But she doesn't remember anything and doesn't talk well enough to give us anything anyway."

"I noticed she had a doll," Bryant asked. "Did the FBI buy it for her?"

"According to what I was told, she had it when she was picked up."

"Okay," the woman suggested, "let's go look at the doll."

With Bryant leading the way, the two left the crime scene and marched down three doors. A knock brought a stern looking woman about thirty to the entry, who, when told what they needed, retrieved the doll.

"What are you looking for?" Morris demanded as Bryant took the twelve-inch toy and ran her hands it from head to toe. Finding nothing in the clothing, the woman shook the doll.

"Do you hear that?" she asked.

"Yeah," he replied, "something's loose inside."

Bryant grabbed the doll's head and twisted it to the left. A half turn positioned the head where she could gently pull it from the body. After peering inside, she turned it over and a key fell into her hands. After handing the body and head back to Morris, she said, "Put it back together."

As the man went to work, Bryant studied the key. It was small and stamped onto the top was 25.

"This fits a locker," she noted as Morris handed the doll back to the hired babysitter. "Now we have to find out where the locker is."

"Must be the bowling alley," the woman matter-a-factly announced. "That's the only place in Taylorville where you can rent a locker."

By the time Morris had issued a thanks, Bryant was to the stairs. He finally caught up with her just as she strolled out the hotel's front door. The next two blocks were covered at a brisk pace. Once inside the crowded, smoky bowling alley, the woman glanced past the twelve lanes and all those playing, beyond the snack bar, to a wall of lockers six feet high and twenty wide on the far wall. Ignoring everything except what was in her line of sight, she resolutely crossed the room glancing intently at the green cubicles until she found the number she needed. Inserting the key, she turned it to the right and the door popped open.

"There's the new bag," she pointed out.

As Morris leaned over her shoulder, the woman opened the zipper at the top of the duffle bag. Stacks of freshly printed green paper greeted her.

"How much would say is in there?" Bryant asked.

"If all the bills are twenties," the man suggested, "perhaps as much as fifty grand. There's an envelope off to the side What's in it."

Bryant retrieved the white letter-sized envelope and ran her fingernail under the edge of the flap. Once she'd broken the seal, she reached in.

"A ticket to a St. Louis Browns' baseball game," she announced, "and a note card."

"What's it say?"

She glanced over the typed message before handing it to the agent. After reading it, he leaned close and whispered, "This is a payoff of some kind. She's supposed to take the cash to the game and set it beneath her seat. The man to her right will take it. She's then supposed to tell him the rest will be delivered when the job is done."

"The game's on Tuesday," Bryant added.

"So," Morris added, "It's not a kidnapping or a lover's quarrel gone bad. There's something big at play here. Good thing the locals called us in."

"Yeah," she agreed as she dropped the note and ticket back into the bag, zipped it shut, slid it out of the locker and headed to the door. If she could solve this one, then J. Edgar would really owe her.

"You know," she added, "what are the odds of a delivery woman named Brown making the payoff at a St. Louis Browns game?"

CHAPTER 13

Sunday, July 19, 1942
9:45 AM
A stake out in Taylorville, Illinois

The five team members sat in their rented Ford and watched the café. Behind the wheel was a frumpy looking Helen Meeker, in the front passenger seat was Clay Barnes, filling the back were Dizzy Vance, Gail Worel, and Becca Bobbs.

"You're sure they've checked out of the hotel?" Meeker asked while never taking her eyes off the eatery's front door.

Vance, dressed as a farmer, chimed in, "I watched them pay their bill and heard the man say they were grabbing some breakfast before hitting the road."

"Okay," Meeker announced, moving her head until her eyes met Bobbs. "We're all in the same place for the first time. Now is the right time to catch us up on all you've dug up."

Bobbs nodded. "I think we pretty much all know by now that the woman is Teresa Bryant. Here are few more things I found out about her this morning. She got her job at the FBI through a relationship she had with an agent named James Killpatrick. She was with Killpatrick when he was shot and killed picking up the kidnapping victim … Amy Boatright … in Indiana. Supposedly Bryant's a file clerk, but as Mr. Hoover trusts her to go on the road, which file clerks never do, I have to believe she is much more. So we can assume that she's not just taking notes but also assisting Agent Chet Morris."

"What do you know about Morris?" Vance asked. "He's an agent I've never run into."

"I actually worked with him a couple of times," Bobbs explained. "He brought some stuff to the lab for me to go over. He's a good guy, a straight shooter, who has a wonderful sense of humor. Graduated from Princeton, so he's bright as well."

"What about our victim?" Meeker cut in.

"Not much new there. We know she's O'Toole's sister, but the rest is kind of fuzzy. We think she was born in 1918 in Ireland and came to the US with her family a year later … that's what the 1920 census indicates … that would make her twenty-four. She was married to Edward Brown in Kansas City when she was eighteen. He was in the army so they moved around a lot. He died on Wake Island. At that time, she was living in San Diego. There is no record of her from the time she left California four months ago and when she showed up at the rooming house. Stranger yet, there are no records concerning Angela. She must be about three and Brown was in San Antonio around that time, but there is no birth certificate Alison's sources could dig up. Plus, according to Army records, Edward's only dependent was his wife."

"So," Barnes cracked, "Maybe she kidnapped the kid and it went south when she tried to collect."

Vance, his eyes still watching the café, offered another theory. "What if Jaws was behind the kidnapping? Maybe she was holding the kid for him."

"You Americans love to complicate a mystery," Worel suggested. "The girl wouldn't have told us her name was Brown if it wasn't and, when I had her, Angela told me Mrs. Brown was her mother. So she pretty much had to have been living with the woman for a long time."

"You like tossing water on a good fire," Barnes cracked.

"Gail's right," Meeker added. "Besides, I'm more interested in who Bryant is than Brown at this point. Did Alison's contacts find out anything about her past?"

Bobbs shrugged. "They found three different pasts and none of them seem real. It's almost like she appeared out of nowhere and somehow caught Hoover's eye."

"The FBI," Barnes suggested, "must consider her valuable enough to muddy things to keep anyone from tracing her background. I doubt if Teresa Bryant is really her name."

"How do you know," Meeker asked, "that she's not using Hoover? We checked all three backgrounds because we were suspicious due only to something she said to Fister. Hoover had no reason to do that. What if we had simply checked the official records through the FBI, what would we think of her then?"

"The background on Bryant the FBI has is clean," Bobbs added. "On that one, her references were top shelf and her educational background spotless."

"Then," Meeker suggested, "I doubt if Hoover even dug for anything else. So my guess is she's playing them."

"Why?" Barnes asked. "What's the purpose?"

"Hoover has his enemies in both organized crime and politics. Bryant might be there to destroy him. What better way to get to a powerful man than through a woman who makes Heddy Lamarr look like a wallflower?"

"So," Bobbs added, "where does Fister figure into this mess?"

"That seems obvious," Barnes noted. "Reggie and Bryant have the same boss. Bryant's boss is Hoover, so Reggie must have been paid by the FBI to find out what we were doing. When Alistar died, they pulled him away from us, possibly worried his cover had been blown or perhaps they decided that we were not the kind of team the FBI needed to worry about. Now Hoover might be a step ahead of us; maybe he actually knows who Bryant really is, sent her to Taylorville, a small town well off the beaten path, to have Reggie take her out. But then Dizzy stepped in and turned the tables."

Vance shook his head. "Then where is he now?"

Barnes frowned. "My hunch is that Bryant took him out and got rid of the body."

"Your logic goes south in a hurry," Meeker explained. "If your scenario were spot on, Bryant would be on the lamb because she'd know that Hoover is gunning for her, but she's sticking with the case. So she and Fister are connected in another way and Hoover didn't set her up to be knocked off. So J. Edgar is more in the dark than we are."

"They're coming out," Vance noted.

Meeker reached down and touched the starter button. As she did, the Ford quietly came to life. She waited at the curb for Morris to pull out onto the main street. When he was fifty feet down the road, she eased out into the road to follow.

"They're heading south on Highway 48," Barnes pointed out.

"So," Meeker added, "that likely means they're headed to St. Louis. The question becomes, are they going to grab a plane and fly back east or have they found something involving Peggy Brown's murder and are chasing down that lead?"

As the two cars continued down the state road, Bobbs opted to pose one final question. "What happened to Fister?"

No one hazarded a guess.

CHAPTER 14

Sunday, July 19, 1942
10:15 PM
The Gulf of Mexico

The U-boat's repairs were solid enough to get the old boat running but far short of complete. Hence, Henry Reese was no longer on a cruise; he was now just inching along toward Mexico. He likely could have swum to his destination faster. As the visitor stood on the deck glancing out into the night sky, his thoughts were of England and the young woman who'd recently help save Hans Holsclaw's career as an underground leader.

Gail Worel was an enigma. He'd never met anyone like her. One on hand, she was the definition of military precision cloaked in British reserve. She possessed movie star looks that she carried with almost regal bearing. She was both imaginative and no nonsense. She was blunt, honest, and direct. And, on their brief time away from the business of war, she proved to be warm, tender, and loving. Even after days on and under the sea, her kiss still lingered on lips and her touch still burned his cheek. Thus, her memory lingered like a powerful perfume.

"You look lost in thought," Fitz Klein noted as he joined the American.

"Yeah," Reese admitted. "I was just thinking about someone I wish I'd never met?"

The commander shook his head, "It must be a woman."

"And what a woman she is," Reese admitted. "Until I met her, I was sure I loved another woman and if I lived through this mess, I'd track down that woman from my past and declare how much I loved her. But …"

"Then you met the second woman," Klein cracked.

Reese turned to face his host. "You can't love two women."

The commander laughed. "In war, you will discover you think you love almost every woman you meet. You see, we need to find a bond and hang onto it because we know that tomorrow we might die. And none of us wants to die without feeling we are loved. If there is no one to come home to, then why go home? I may have muddled that up some, but I think you see where I going. There has to be a reason to live and could there be a better reason than the love of a woman?"

Reese didn't get it. Was Klein telling him he wasn't in love or that he was only in love because his life was constantly on the line? As amazing as Gail was, he could still see the look in Helen's eyes that last night her saw her in Germany.

"None of us may get home," the commander wryly noted. "The old boat's in bad shape. We took a pounding. Right now we're limping along on guts and imagination and both of those have their limits. So you may never have to make that choice you seemingly don't want to make."

Reese looked back out into the waters of the Gulf. "What happens if the sub quits and you can't fix it? I'm guessing you can't call a tow truck and haul her back to the garage for an overhaul."

"No," he admitted, "It's not that easy. If it dies, we'll try to get as close to shore as we can and then we sink it or blow it up."

"You're a long way from home, my friend. So, without the U-boat, how do you get back to your family?"

"We aren't going to get home in this tub," Klein explained. "We can't dive. Hence, we are a sitting duck. Tomorrow or the next day someone will spot us. They will radio in and the American Navy or Coast Guard will go hunting. It will be like going after a badly wounded animal … the hunt will be short."

"And what happens then?" Reese asked.

"We'll put up a fight, shoot our deck guns and try to fire a few torpedoes, but we likely won't hit anything."

"Why not give up? Why not just wave the white flag and surrender?"

"That's not in our character," Klein noted. "If we're spotted, we'll fight until we sink. So our time is running out and so is yours."

"I'm not sure how to take that."

"If you really are Nigel Armstrong," the commander noted, "and I still have my doubts on that, then you can't afford to be captured. If the Allies get you, then you'll be executed. If they get the crew, we will sit out the war in a POW camp. So you don't need to be here when the fireworks start."

"So does that mean I walked the plank?"

Klein shook his head. "No, we'll be off the Yucatan in Mexico by morning. When we see the shore, we'll put you in a dingy and let you take your treasure and paddle to safety."

"Why's my getting away so important?" Reese asked. "I figured you had orders to kill me if I didn't come through with the information Hitler needed."

"I had orders to kill you the moment you gave me the name," Klein cracked. "This was the end of the line for you. The loot was simply a loan that I'd take home with me and give back to the government."

"Then why let me go now?" Reese demanded as he stared into the commander's blue eyes. "Why not just follow your orders?"

"I think you know," came the quick reply. "And it has nothing to do with the treasure chest or the fact you aren't going to give me the name Hitler wants."

The two remained mute, their uneasy friendship causing both of them to consider thoughts they likely wouldn't admit to having. Five minutes became ten and ten became twenty and they remained silent looking out into the night.

"I likely will never know your real name," Klein announced, "but I'm sure you're not the man I was supposed to pick up. You have too much character to sell out your country and it's that character I'm depending upon to share what I know with the Allies."

Reese shook his head, "You're assuming a lot."

"I'm assuming nothing," he shot back. "And if things had gone as planned when you had gotten off this boat, I fully expected the name you'd have given me for the underground leader would have not be the right one." He smiled, "But I'm also sure you know who the real leader is."

"Fritz, whose side are you on?"

"My family's side and that's where things are very complicated for me. Now you need to get below and get your stuff ready. I'll come get you when we come close enough to Mexico to launch you toward whatever it is you're chasing."

The commander turned and walked back toward the con and Reese's eyes followed the famed undersea assassin each step of the way. For this man who seemed to possess a strange combination of a lust for blood mixed with great moral character, the war was about to be finished. Klein would never again see his wife and children. He would never know if the photo he'd entrusted to Reese would ever be seen and if the story behind it would ever be told. Like millions of others, his life would end with the world upside down. There were too many good men dying each day and, in a very strange way, Reese understood that Fritz Klein was one of those. In spite of the uniform he was wearing, he was a good man.

CHAPTER 15

Sunday, July 19, 1942
3:45 PM
Farm outside of Springfield, Illinois

Fredrick Bauer was a man who expected his orders to be followed to the letter. Thus, the news Fister had just given him did not set well. Yet as Teresa Bryant had called in and explained she was not in Taylorville when his hired gun arrived in the quiet Midwestern city, coming up empty made sense. Plus, the fact Bryant called in two more times to give him updates on the case seem to prove she was at least willing to keep him in the loop. These calls might even prove she was coming back into the fold. So perhaps having her alive and breathing might be a good thing after all. The news he wanted to hear might not have as been as good the news he got.

Bauer glanced at Fister as the man nervously sat and played with the ring he'd been given before being sent out on the job.

This was not the same confident young man he'd groomed into a cold, calculating killing machine. Dressed in slacks and a t-shirt, his hair uncombed and an ugly gash on his cheek, he had none of the cocky presence and charm that had once made him so valuable. The question that had to be answered was, "Would he ever get back to being the man he had been?" If he didn't, then Fister would likely be of very little use to Bauer and his work. So he might just have to depend upon the unpredictable Bryant until he could find another man to replace Fister.

The guest must have felt his host's gaze because he quickly slipped the ring back into his pocket and sat straight in his chair. Yet, while with trying to maintain good posture, Fister still looked like a frightened teen who had been taken to the principal's office. If anything he seemed worse than he had before being sent to Taylorville.

"If I could have," Fister whispered apologetically, "I would have. You can count on me."

Bauer frown, the old Fister would have no offered excuses or apologized. He would have jumped up and blamed someone else for his failures. The fire was gone and perhaps it would never be restored.

"It wasn't your fault," Bauer suggested. "I didn't think they'd get out of Taylorville as soon as they did. Besides, the fact she checked in might make Bryant valuable to me after all. It was likely just as well you didn't get a chance to knock her off."

"Good," the guest announced, seemingly relieved.

"Can you cook?" Bauer demanded.

"I'm not too bad in the kitchen," came the quick response.

"Then scramble some eggs, make some toast, and take it out to the barn. There's a little girl staying in one of the rooms in the lab and she's likely hungry. Be gentle with her too. She's experienced a tough last few days."

"Little girl?"

"Yeah about three," Bauer replied. "She'll be staying with us for a while until I can work out plans for her future. She's valuable, so treat her with as much care I do that stuff in the room below the house."

Bauer sat as his desk as Fister got up and left the room. Once the tall man heard pans rattling in the kitchen, he got up, moved to the bookcase, worked the secret code and opened the door to the treasure room. A few seconds later, a woman walked up the hidden stairs and into the study.

"You kept me down there long enough," she complained. Pushing a loose strand of hair from her face, she ambled over to the chair Fister had just vacated and took a seat. Once the matronly middle-aged woman crossed her left leg over her right and placed her hands over her knee, she made an observation. "I don't know why you don't bury her. It creeps me out looking at her."

"I can't let her go," Bauer explained.

"And Fred, that's your weakness. At some point, your not allowing her to just fade away will lead to your downfall. And the fact you're obsessed with this Meeker woman because she looks like her is just sick. Meeker is someone who needs to be taken out. If I ever meet her, I'll do just that and someday you'll thank me for it too."

"Don't lecture me," he suggested. "Those who do always wish they hadn't."

"Okay, let's move on, but don't forget my warning. Now, why don't you bring me up to speed on what was behind my mission."

"That little girl I grabbed," Bauer began.

"The Brown woman's daughter," the visitor noted.

"Well, she's Jaws O'Toole's niece. I'm not sure how much O'Toole knows about me so that kid's my insurance policy. As long as I have her, I can keep him on a leash. He's a lot more unpredictable than Carfano."

The woman shrugged. "Then why didn't you grab both of them? Why let one of the twins go?"

"Twice as much trouble to deal with both kids," Bauer explained. "One will do."

"That makes sense," she admitted, "but why did I have to take out the woman?"

Bauer smiled. "Jaws will blame the hit on people loyal to Carfano. He will start taking out anyone who was close to the dead mob leader. So, just in case any of them know anything about me, they will be silenced."

"So you're tying up loose ends," she suggested.

"I'm not sure they're loose," he explained, "but because I don't know, it was necessary to convince O'Toole to do a little house cleaning. He will be fast and brutal."

"So why order me back here?" the woman asked. "Why didn't you let me go home? Do you have another assignment for me?"

Bauer got up, moved around his desk and stood in front of his guest. "Obviously, I want you to keep feeding me information that your husband shares with you and to photograph and forward any plans he brings home from work. But I also need for you to get to know and watch a woman who works for the FBI. Her name is Teresa Bryant. She's on the stuff and is supposed to be working for me, but her backstory washed out. I really don't know who she is and who's she's playing for."

"You slipped up," the woman cracked. "I told you time and time again to do your homework."

"Well, I usually do." He returned to his desk, opened a drawer and pulled out two photographs. After momentarily staring at the images, he pushed them toward his guest.

"She's pretty," the woman noted. "In fact, she is beautiful. She must have theatrical sense about her too. In this one photo, she dressed up like an Indian from the last century."

He nodded. "The one in your right hand is a picture of the woman I know as Teresa Bryant. The other picture was taken decades ago."

"But the two women are the same right down the mole on the right cheek."

"I know," Bauer admitted.

"How?" the visitor asked.

"I have no idea," he replied. "But that's why you're going to get to know her. So have a party and make sure she's invited. Ask her to come to your book club meetings. Find ways to run into her every chance you get. Learn as much as you can and then share it with me." He paused and rubbed his brow before adding, "And when the time is right, I'll have you kill her."

131

"Even my being the wife of General Root doesn't mean I can convince this woman to come to my parties and clubs, much less open up to me."

"I know," Bauer admitted, "but I'll give her the assignment of getting to know you too. So that should make it much easier. Now, before I sneak you out of here and get you back to Washington, who were the folks who found you in Brown's room? I had it set up for the local cops to make the discovery."

"I never saw most of them," she explained. "They kept me blindfolded. There was one fat guy who spent some time with me, but I'd never see him before. I will tell you this, they knew who I was and were doing their best to protect me. The fat guy informed me that when I was out they gave me a paraffin test. So it's good I always wear gloves when I do those little assignments for you. But why did you want to play it like I'd been framed?"

"You were spotted in town," he explained.

"Yeah," Root replied. "An old college friend did see me and she called my husband."

"So have you talked to the general?"

"I told him my sister needed to go to Taylorville on business. He bought it."

"As long as it keeps your cover," Bauer noted, "then it's fine."

"It's not easy being your sister."

"But it does have a payoff," he assured her, "and you just spent some time looking over some of the goods. There's a lot more to come."

"Fine," Root shot back, "but give me a break from knocking people off for a while. I'm behind on my reading."

He laughed. "You're as cold as I am."

"Fred, it's in our blood. Now let's get me home."

CHAPTER 16

Sunday, July 19, 1942
10:15 PM
Regis Hotel, St. Louis, Missouri

"Seriously," Teresa Bryant announced as she looked out from the fifth floor of the Regis Hotel, "I can pull this off. We know what we're supposed to do. Brown was to get into the game with her ticket, sit in the seat, and a man in the next seat was going to take the bag from her."

"What if he knows the woman?" Chet Morris asked.

"Then he likely doesn't sit down," she explained, "and it's a dry run. Nothing can really happen to me. It's a ballpark for heaven's sake. There are witnesses everywhere. So either it works or it doesn't."

"But if he knows you," the man argued, "and he doesn't come up, then we might never find out what this is all about."

"How are you going to find out if we don't try? I'm going to wear a hat with a veil over my face; he'll have to get close to determine if I'm Peggy Brown, so that means if you keep your eyes open you'll spot him if he sits by me and takes the bag or not. As I see it, this is a can't miss opportunity to close this case and have Hoover crown you as a hero."

"Maybe."

"And," she continued, "After we spot the guy, we tail him out of the park and see where he goes. He'll take us to whoever is behind this. I can just see the award the FBI will give you now. Maybe you'll get a raise too."

"Okay," he agreed, "we'll do it your way. But the game's not until Tuesday. How do we kill two days?"

Bryant smiled and batted her long lashes. "This town is filled with great restaurants and night spots. So we do a little shopping, find the right clothes and then we let our hair down. I'll bet you're great dancer and I can hardly wait for you to take me in your big, strong arms and spin me across the dance floor." She waltzed across the room to Morris, leaned close enough for him to smell her perfume and purred, "Now, why don't you go back to your room and get some sleep. Tomorrow, we're going to pack a month's worth of fun into one day. I'll promise you'll never forget a second of it."

She opened the door and pointed to the hall. When he balked, she reached up and kissed him lightly on the lips. "There will be enough time for that tomorrow. I need my rest now. So get moving."

Though his eyes begged him to stay, the gentleman that defined his true character pushed him out and, as soon as he stepped into the hall, Bryant closed and locked the door. She stood by the entry, waiting for five minutes before opening it slightly and looking out. The hall was now empty. Moving back to the bed, she retrieved her large purse, checked her make up in the mirror, slipped on a light blue jacket that matched her skirt, exited the room, and made her way down the hall to the stairwell. After glancing back to make sure no one was looking, she hurried down the four flights and into the lobby. Surveying the large room, she noted a bellboy, the clerk, and one man, likely a guest. The latter was sitting in an oversized chair reading a newspaper and the others were visiting at the main desk. Satisfied none of the three were looking her direction, she stepped across the side of the lobby to a row of phone booths positioned on the near wall. Once in, she reached into her purse and retrieved a handful of change. She then called the operator and gave her a number. It took three minutes for the call to be completed and the phone on the other end to ring.

"Yes."

"It's Bryant."

"Are you in Chicago?" the man demanded.

"No, I'm in St. Louis. I need some information."

"I thought you said you were in Chicago the last time you called; why are you in St. Louis?"

"I go where Morris goes," she shot back, happy that Baker had bought her other story. "Now about that information."

"And why ask me?"

"Because, Fred, you're the puppet master. You have more contacts than the FBI. And when you found out I was accompanying Morris to Taylorville, I'm sure you started digging. So give me something I can use to suck Hoover a bit closer to my web."

The line was quiet for a few seconds before Bauer popped a question. "Does Hoover realize the woman spinning that web is a Black Widow?"

"I can't be," she argued, "I've never been married."

"That's not the story you gave me on that plane."

"And you've proven that story was a lie," she quipped. "Now, do you know anything about why that Peggy Brown woman was murdered?"

The man didn't respond. In fact, if she hadn't been able to hear his breathing, she would have sworn he'd hung up. Finally, after what seemed like an eternity, Bauer volunteered some information. "The woman who was shot is the sister of the mob leader Jaws O'Toole. This likely signals a war between Carfano's old allies and the new power behind the Midwestern Syndicate."

"Okay," she replied, "Hoover will love that. Thanks. You got anything else?"

"I have lots, but that's all I'm sharing." She heard him lick his lips before demanding, "Now who are you?"

Bryant laughed, "You just keep digging."

His reply was cold and chilling. "I could dig up every cemetery in this country and never find your grave."

"You have to die to be buried," she noted.

"I know," he assured her.

Bryant smiled as she put the receiver back into its carriage. Bauer had taken the bait and before long he would begin to choke on it.

CHAPTER 17

Monday, July 20, 1942
6:50 PM
Stakeout in St. Louis

Gail Worel studied the phone as if believing her gaze would make it ring. It didn't.

Across the hotel room, Becca Bobbs smiled. "I thought you Brits were supposed to have great patience and reserve."

"Some do," the sergeant announced, "I once thought I did as well, but this is driving me crazy. We should have gotten notification of where we need to be to pick up our man and the package by now. The fact we haven't heard likely means there are problems."

"Well," the Bobbs noted, "as I understand it, the message will go through to the President's office to Alison and she will contact us. That means the phone will ring when the word comes in. Until that happens we stick to this case."

"But this case means nothing compared to …"

"Wait a minute," a suddenly stern Bobbs announced with a wave of a hand, "a child lost its mother and a woman is dead. Even when the world has gone mad and people are killed in waves, those lives still have to mean something. We can't get to the point where death makes no impact."

"But what happens when the call comes through?" Worel demanded. "Do we break this off and get back our mission or do we stay here." She swept the now dyed blonde hair away from her face. "I'll tell you this … I'm going."

"You love this guy," Bobbs announced. "That's what this is all about. This isn't about the jewels or taking out the Nazi's top U-boat captain, this is about reuniting with a man."

"What if it is?"

"I'm tempted to quote Bogart in *Casablanca*," Bobbs continued, "because he got it right. The desires of two people don't matter right now. There is something much larger at work here."

"How would you know?" Worel demanded. "Are you in love?"

There was no immediate answer. Instead, the other woman in the room stood, walked over to the window and looked out at the St. Louis street scene playing out below.

"You are in love aren't you?"

Bobbs turned, "I might be, but we both decided we couldn't push that agenda right now. You see, the work we're doing is more important than what we're feeling toward each other. So we've put things on hold. I think you need to put them on hold too."

142

"Is that fair?"

"There're lots of things in life that aren't fair," Bobbs argued. "That little girl losing her mother isn't fair either. And let's not even talk about Helen watching the Nazis kill the man she loved."

"What?" Worel demanded. "I knew Helen had lost someone, but I had no idea she'd seen him die?"

"He wasn't her lover," Bobbs sadly noted. "They had a history and they were both just starting to figure out they really loved each other." She paused and shook her head. "I likely shouldn't be sharing this with you. It's none of my business."

"What's the harm?" Worel asked. "If I'm going to working with Helen, I need to know her as something more than just a team leader. I need to see her as a person. She doesn't seem to let that part of her show much."

"Maybe she quit being a person on that night," Bobbs suggested.

"What night?"

"The night that …" her voice trailed off and she turned once again to look out the window.

"Becca, what's this all about?"

"He and Helen had worked together when she was assigned to the FBI before the war. When the President formed this team, they came back together as a part of it. In a sense, they changed roles. She was now his superior where it had once been the other way around."

"How did he die?"

"We were on a mission behind enemy lines," Bobbs explained, her pained expression proving she didn't like revisiting this memory. "Things didn't work out the way they were supposed to. Henry gave his life to make sure Helen and I got away."

"Henry's kind of a noble name," Worel noted as she considered the irony of the man she cared deeply about having the same name.

"He was a noble guy," came the quick response. "He was good looking, cool, and giving. He put others first. He was a great talker but a better listener. And he respected women. He didn't treat us like second-class citizens or dolls to be played with. He saw us as equals."

"That sounds like the guy on that U-boat."

"Really?"

"Yeah, they even have the same name. He's an American working with the underground. According to Russell Strickland, he's pretty much Superman. I kind of feel like he's Cary Grant, Clark Gable, and Jimmy Stewart all wrapped into one person."

"Small world," Bobbs noted. "We've worked with Strickland as well. And about your guy, he sounds like he could be Henry Reese's twin."

Worel's eyes went from looking dreamily into space to staring a hole in the other woman. Had Bobbs just said what she thought she'd heard? Surely not! Yet, there was no way there could be two Henry Reeses in this war. Getting up, she walked over to her purse, opened it, reached into a side pocket and retrieved a photo. She studied it for a moment and as she did her heart skipped a beat. Taking a deep breath, she strolled back to where Bobbs stood by the window.

"Is this Helen's Henry?" the Brit asked.

Worel was praying with a zeal unlike any she'd ever known as she handed the photo to Bobbs. That prayer intensified as the woman silently studied the image. The prayer ended when the Brit noted the America's stunned expression.

"How did you get Henry's picture," Bobbs demanded. "And why pretend you didn't know about the man Helen had loved and lost?"

Then it was true, the man she loved was the same person Helen Meeker loved. Unknowingly she had come to America to reunite two lovers and likely end her own dreams of romance. As a million different emotions flooded her mind, Bobbs grabbed Worel and shook her.

"Where did you get this picture?"

"That's my Henry," Worel whispered, "and he's not dead."

"He can't be alive," Bobbs shot back.

"I don't know why or how," Worel admitted, "but he is alive. I promise you on the king's name, he never told me about being shot nor did he mention the mission you just spoke about. We didn't really talk about what we did before we met, we just enjoyed the moments we had."

The American woman glanced toward the phone.

"Now, Becca, you want it to ring as badly as I do."

"I guess I do, but …"

"But do you tell Helen?" Worel cut her off and asked. "I'll leave that up to you. But, if this turns out the way I figure it will, I'd like to have that picture back. Beyond a few memories, it might just be all I take back with me to England."

"We can't tell Helen," Bobbs suggested.

"Why not?"

"What if that call never comes? What if he dies before he gets to his rendezvous point? I don't want to see her heart break twice. I just don't know if she could take that."

"If he does get back," Worel whispered, "one of us is going to be hurt. If he doesn't, both of us will. Either way, it hardly seems fair."

Bobbs nodded. "Helen and Clay's shift watching Morris and Bryant will end in an hour. We'll take over then. Just promise me you won't say anything to her about Henry."

"I won't."

The reason Worel so readily agreed to keep quiet had nothing to do with possibly setting Meeker up for a second heartbreak; it was all about her being able to pretend that Henry Reese was all hers for at least another day. She glanced down at the picture Bobbs had returned. Why had she fallen so hard so fast? Why? Why? Why?

CHAPTER 18

Monday, July 20, 1942
3:50 PM
Jim O'Toole's palatial home on
Lake Michigan just outside Chicago, Illinois

O'Toole liked the name Jaws. He'd earned as a kid in Ireland when he'd knocked out kids in schoolyard fights with a short right to the chin. A few years later, he'd turned his ability to deliver blows and inflict injury into a successful career as a boxer. The fight game brought him to New York. A year and ten wins later, O'Toole began to understand that knocking out lugs in ring didn't pay nearly as well as being an enforcer for the Big Apple's Irish mob. Blessed with even more brains than brawn, as an enforcer he carefully moved up in the syndicate finally ending up in Chicago in 1940 as Rudy Carfano's number two man. With the death of the prince, O'Toole claimed the throne as the underworld's new ruler. With his reputation for taking no prisoners, no one had challenged his right to the crown.

A white, nine-bedroom stone home with a dynamic view of Lake Michigan was his palace. Built in 1922 by a Windy City banker, O'Toole bought it from its second owner, a baseball player who'd thrown his arm out. Upon moving in, Jaws left the home just as it was except for adding a tall stone and iron fence and bringing in hired guards with dogs. The latter patrolled the five acres of grounds twenty-four hours a day. After all, in his line of work you could never be too careful.

With a cigar in one hand and a Scotch in the other, O'Toole roamed from the room's huge living room out into a twenty-foot wide hall to a large study. The walls were lined with books that had come with the house. If it had been cushioned and had pockets, the room's mahogany desk could have been used as a regulation pool table; it was likely a dozen cows died just to cover the nine high-backed reading chairs setting by the brass floor lamps that had been placed in a semicircle around the desk. Walking over to a table, the big man tapped his cigar ashes into a crystal dish and eased down into one of the oversized green chairs. He'd no more than gotten comfortable when he heard the doorbell, followed by the butler's steps across the hall's marble floor. A few minutes later, a dapperly dressed small man strolled into the gangster's lair.

Stanford Poole was five-feet-eight and weighed no more than one-fifty. He was about fifty, gray-headed, wore a blue suit, white shirt, and solid blue tie, and had wire-rimmed glasses perched on his nose. He looked much more like a university dean than O'Toole's most trusted torpedo.

"You have something for me?" Poole asked

148

"Take a seat, Stan," the host announced pointing to a chair directly across from him. "I need you to go to St. Louis. There's a down payment for services that's being delivered by a woman and I want you to watch the transaction."

"That sounds like a job for a flunky," the guest observed.

"Normally it would be," O'Toole explained. "But in this case, the delivery woman is someone important to me."

"Then why not have her bring it to you herself. Why do I have to pick it up?"

"You're not there to pick the package up," O'Toole announced, "You're there to see who does. This deal was set up by Carfano. Someone in government circles was doing a favor for him. I want to do know who it is. So you follow the payoff guy back to the source and let me know the name of the top cat and how much pull he's got."

"Why have you're the woman deliver the loot? Why not me or one of the boys?"

"Because this guy has no connection to me," O'Toole explained. "So none of my gang needs to be a part of it." The big man leaned forward in his chair and whispered, "The delivery woman is named Peggy Brown. She's my sister."

Poole shook his head. "I didn't know you had a sister. I thought all your relatives were either in Ireland or dead."

"Yeah," he admitted, "that's my story. And now that Rudy's dead, you're the only person who knows she's my sister. Sharing that information shows just how much I trust you. But if you tell anyone, I will not hesitate to kill you. Understand?"

"Yes."

"Anyway, I keep her out of the spotlight for her safety, but on this deal I needed someone I can trust. And except for you and Peggy, I don't trust anyone with that kind of money. Carfano promised a woman would deliver the payoff, so that's why she's doing it and you're not."

The mobster reached into his shirt pocket and pulled out four tickets. As he extended his arm toward his guest, he explained, "These tickets will put you and the guys in key places where you can watch the payoff."

Poole took the tickets, studied each of them and put them in his pocket. As he did, his boss continued.

"You've never seen my sister. There's a photo on the table beside you. Slip it out of the frame and take it with you. Also, have one of your guys take a camera and shoot a photo of the guy who meets her. If we lose him, we might be able to trace him through the picture."

"Anything else?"

"I don't want any gunplay. Just follow the guy and see who he takes the money too. It will likely be a complicated transfer, so I think it'd be best if each of you had your own car. That way you can tag team if necessary. Come back here and tell me what you find out."

"Got it."

"And my sister's got twin daughters. When I met her a few days ago in Taylorville, I told her not to bring them to the park."

"You were in Taylorville?"

"Yeah, a week ago today? Why?"

150

Poole shrugged. "There was a murder in Taylorville about that same time. It was all over the papers."

"I don't pay much attention to the papers," O'Toole explained, "and I certainly don't care about murders unless I order them. Anybody you know get bumped off?"

"The papers didn't have a name. So for all I know, it was just some dame."

"Ah," the mobster laughed, "likely a gal who was caught by her husband with her boyfriend. Must have happened after I left because no one was talking about it when I was there."

"You said something about your sister's daughters?"

"Yeah, I want them to have the best of everything. I don't want them around the rackets. So as soon as this little gig is finished, I'm sending my sister and those girls to a place I bought in a small town in Florida. No one will ever connect them with me and they'll be able to grow up like just normal people." He took a puff on his cigar and looked back to his guest. "How does that sound to you?"

"Like heaven."

O'Toole chuckled. "Get going. You need to have your crew down to St. Louis and in place for tomorrow afternoon's game."

Wordlessly, Poole got up and quickly moved out of the room, down the hall and to the front door. Once again alone, O'Toole picked up the latest issues of *Time*, flipped back to the movie reviews and searched for a film he might want to catch later in the evening.

CHAPTER 19

Tuesday, July 21, 1942
1:05 PM
Sportsman's Park, St. Louis, Missouri

Sportsman's Park was a quaint baseball venue that had been serving St. Louis since 1908. About half the capacity of Yankee Stadium, the park on Sullivan Avenue had the rare distinction of hosting not one but two major league teams. The Cardinals were traditionally one of the best squads in either league and the Browns were usually one of the worst. So while many of the Redbird's games were packed with thirty thousand screaming fans, their American League counterparts usually played to a few thousand loyal souls. Today, as the Browns, or Brownies as the locals often called them, took on Connie Mack's Philadelphia Athletics, the ballpark's vendors almost outnumbered the ticket-buying patrons.

"Why would they come here?" Meeker asked as they watched Bryant and Morris get out of the car and head toward the stadium.

"Why would they do anything they did yesterday?" Barnes added. "We followed them into shops, department stores, and two restaurants. They bought, ate, and even went to a club and danced for hours. She was hanging all over him. If they'd danced any closer, she could have worn his suit coat." He glanced back at Bobbs. "If this is an undercover assignment, I should draw this kind of job. Spending money, living the high life, holding a beautiful woman in my arms on the dance floor, kissing her good night and then going to a baseball game, Helen, I'm up for all those things if you need a volunteer."

"You'd need a partner," Bobbs suggested.

"Focus, gang," Meeker chimed in. Clay, why don't you get us five tickets; that'll fulfill the last part of your fantasy. Meanwhile, we'll try to watch where they go when they enter."

As the man hurried across the parking lot, Bobbs made an observation. "That's a big bag Bryant's carrying and I'm not talking about her purse. Why would she need both of those things?"

"And," Worel added, "look at her hat. Do people in America still wear veils like that?"

"Dizzy," Meeker suggested, "you keep your eye on the FBI agent, the rest of us will follow Bryant. They're going in the gate on the first base side. Looks like Clay has noticed that as well. Hopefully, he'll get seats in the same area."

With Meeker, dressed in a light tan suit, matching heels and a fedora styled hat tilted toward the right, leading the way, the team arrived at the gate at the same time as Barnes. As soon as they were on the concourse, they split up with the still blonde Worel paired with the team leader.

"Gail, start looking around. No more people than are here, we should be able to find her pretty quickly."

"Already have! She's in the first row behind that little building."

Meeker smiled. "It's called a dugout. She's sitting by herself, so where is Morris?"

"After fifty feet to our right," the ever vigilant English woman pointed out, "sitting down in the last row. Mr. Vance has moved just past him."

Meeker honed in on the FBI agent and then her team member. Worel had been spot on. Vance was casually moving along the concourse until he was about fifty feet down the left field line. He then stopped a vendor, bought a bag of peanuts and eased into a seat.

"Where are our seats?" Worel asked.

"It doesn't matter," Meeker assured her. "There will be so few people here it's unlikely we'll take a seat that's been sold. So we'll just move down about five rows and man a position that'll give us a good view of Bryant's box. Then we'll wait to see what happens."

The American led the way down the stairs to the twentieth row and then moved left seven seats. She pointed to seven, and after the Brit had taken her place, Meeker took eight. This spot gave the pair a great vantage point to watch Bryant and still appear to be keeping up with the game. Yet, to make sure their cover as just regular fans was solid, Meeker waved toward a scorecard vendor and purchased a program and a pencil. Next she caught the attention of another hawker and bought two Cokes and a bag of popcorn. And, to make the charade really complete, as the public address announcer began to give the starting lineups, she scribbled the names onto the scorecard. Once that was accomplished, she leisurely searched the stands to see where Bobbs and Barnes had ended up. It didn't take long to spot them, The former was situated about fifty feet beyond and three rows higher than Bryant. Barnes had taken a spot in the second row behind home plate where his position allowed him to easily see the woman and follow her movement while still watching the action of the field.

"Now we wait?" Worel asked between bites of popcorn.

"Yeah," Meeker replied. "And during that time I'll try to explain this crazy game to you."

CHAPTER 21

Tuesday, July 21, 1942
2:15 PM
Sportsman's Park, St. Louis, Missouri

The first six innings clocked in at just over one hour. Thanks to third baseman Clift Harlond and center fielder Wally Judnich, the Browns \charged to a four to one lead in the second inning and then pitcher Al Hollingsworth took control of the game. The Athletics were about to come to bat in the seventh when a man wearing a white short-sleeve shirt and blue slacks slowly ambled down the stairs to the box where Teresa Bryant had been casually watching the game. As Meeker observed the late arriving fan, he stepped past the woman and took a seat. It was apparent Bryant didn't recognize the man and he said nothing to her either.

"Why sit right next to her when there are thousands of seats available?" Worel leaned close and asked.

"That's a really good question," Meeker answered as she glanced toward Chet Morris. The FBI agent, who'd appeared all but asleep a few minutes before, was now staring wide-eyed at the man as well. Something was going on and, based solely on the FBI agent's reaction, this was what they'd evidently been waiting for. Yet, for reasons yet to be revealed, no one moved. For the moment, the newest arrival sat in his chair and watched the game, Bryant did the same and Morris directed his gaze at both of them but also remained fixed to his seat. Had this been a false alarm? Was the guy really just a fan who always sat in that seat?

"Do we wait some more?" Worel asked.

"Yeah," Meeker answered.

In a ballpark that was so quiet you could hear what the players were saying to each other in the infield and detect every call make by the home plate umpire, the public announcer's booming voice echoing through the stadium caused everyone to jump. It so startled the Brit, she spilled what was left of her popcorn.

"Ladies and gentleman, the official attendance for today's game is 7,628. The St. Louis Browns appreciate your attendance and, as a reward, hot dogs are now half price at the concession stands."

"The Browns would have appreciated it more if the crowd had been three times this big," Meeker noted. "Not sure how much longer they will last in St. Louis with this kind of attendance."

"I'm not sure how much longer I'll last on this hard wooden bench either," Worel observed. "It's about time for me to move too."

"At most we have another half hour," Meeker assured her. "So just relax and keep your eye on Bryant."

Over the next seven minutes, everyone in the stands held their place while, on the field, the Athletics managed to bring their second run across the plate. After Hollingsworth shut down the rally, the stadium's organ took over and in unison folks rose for the seventh inning stretch. It was then Bryant made her move. She leaned close to the fan on her right, appeared to say something, then grabbed her purse, stepped out into the aisle and casually strolled to the concourse.

"She left the bag," Worel noted.

"Yeah," Meeker replied.

The team leader didn't move from her seat. Instead, she took a few moments to carefully evaluate the situation. There was no doubt this was a delivery, but for what purpose? Another issue, who would she follow now? Would it be the man with the bag or Bryant? As Barnes stepped toward the aisle, Meeker made a slight wave and caught his attention. When his gaze met hers, she wordlessly directed her eyes toward the man now in possession of the bag. Barnes nodded and sat back in his seat. Confident he would watch the stranger, Meeker stood and turned to follow Bryant.

The raven-haired beauty appeared to be on a mission as she marched past Morris and toward the gate. When the man didn't move, Meeker figured the FBI agent, much like Barnes, was going to trail the collector. That would work to her advantage. As Bryant exited the park through the same gate she'd entered a bit more than an hour and fifteen minutes before, Worel leaned close to the team leader.

"Do you have any guesses?"

"Might be a sting," came the quiet reply. "If that's the case Clay and Dizzy will be close enough to find out what it's about. Let's keep our eyes on the woman."

Thirty steps behind Bryant, Meeker and Worel stepped out of the gate and beyond the confines of Sportsman's Park. As the paired exited, Bryant was just about to cross the street. Then, with no warning, things went south. A green Dodge sedan pulled up, parked at the curb and the driver stepped out. Moving into the shadows, Meeker grabbed Worel and watched to see what would happen next.

From her expression, it seemed Bryant was shocked. When the man pulled a gun from under his suit jacket, it was very obvious things were not going as planned. From the corner of her eye, Meeker detected movement. Glancing to her left, she noted the stranger carrying the bag Bryant had left behind emerging from the ballpark. He was nodding as he quickly approached the car. As he arrived at Bryant's side, the man swung the bag into the back of the woman's head, knocking her to her knees. Undercover or not, it was time for Meeker to do something.

"Stay here," Meeker ordered Worel.

Meeker was reaching into her purse to retrieve her Colt when the situation took another bizarre turn. Just to her right, a small man stepped from behind a parked city bus and began walking toward the two men and Bryant. A split second later, Morris emerged from the stadium, soon followed by Bobbs, Vance, and Barnes. Things were getting very crowded in a hurry.

"Hang on," Meeker whispered to Worel. "With Morris here, we'll let him decide what the next move is. If he needs assistance, we'll move in then."

Who fired that shot was anyone's guess, but the man who'd gotten the bag caught the bullet. When he fell to the ground, blood rushing from the side of his head, the driver of the getaway car grabbed Bryant and dragged her into the Dodge sedan. As everyone held their fire, he rammed the vehicle into gear and pulled out into the street. In seconds, it appeared everyone except Meeker and Worel were racing toward their own vehicles.

"Get the bag," Meeker barked at Worel. "Then join the rest of our team at the car."

Cutting across a half-filled parking lot, Meeker sprinted toward a street that ran perpendicular to the one the driver was using for his escape. She'd looked far enough ahead to see there were barricades about a block down that route. At that point, the driver was going to make a choice of either going right or left. He'd pulled out his gun with his left hand. He likely was still pointing it at Bryant as he drove. That meant he'd be using his right hand to steer the car. Thus, a right turn would be the easiest to accomplish. If she could just get to the middle of the block when he drove by, she could likely get a clean shot.

At first, it was easy to run between cars, but a mid-thirties pick-up looming ahead blocked her path to the street. She didn't have time to run around it, so she leaped upon the Ford's rounded hood and rolled. She came down hard on the pavement with her right knee, ruining a stocking along with earning a sizeable bruise. Dropping down on booth knees, thus shredding a second stocking, she carefully steadied the Colt and squeezed off two rounds. The first hit the man's shoulder and the second struck his head. The car veered to the right and, as his foot had ceased pushing on the acceleration, the vehicle swung into the curb and died. Bouncing up, Meeker sprinted the twenty yards to the car. Just as she arrived, a seemingly healthy and completely calm Bryant stepped out. The two women sized each other up before Meeker lowered her weapon and put it back into her purse.

"Thanks," Bryant announced as casually as if she was acknowledging someone opening a door.

"Are you okay?"

"My ear's are ringing from the blow I took, but I'll be fine." She paused, nodded and smiled. "It's not often I have a ghost riding to my rescue."

"What do you mean?"

"Don't play games," Bryant casually announced, "you're Helen Meeker, the same Helen Meeker who supposedly died in a plane crash earlier this year."

"I don't know what you're talking about," Meeker shot back.

"Looking at you," the woman chirped, "it appears that living forever isn't that hard. In fact, I'm beginning to believe you might know my secret."

"What are you talking about?" Meeker again demanded.

Just like she had the first time, Bryant ignored the question. "I'm also betting you're still in the President's service."

As Meeker continued to eye the woman, Chet Morris drove up. As he got out, Meeker turned and quickly retraced her steps back to their car. The rest of her crew was waiting for her there.

"We need to roll," Meeker announced as she slid in the back seat. As the Ford pulled away with Barnes behind the wheel, she glanced over to Worel. "What's in the bag?"

"A lot of money and a cryptic note."

CHAPTER 21

Tuesday, July 21, 1942
4:15 PM
In a car leaving Sportsman's Park

Like everyone in the Ford sedan, Helen Meeker kept her eyes open to see if anyone was following. After a few miles, when she was sure there were no tails, it was time to figure out their next step. As she saw it, the team only had one choice and that was to go home

"Where to?" Barnes asked.

"The plane," the team leader suggested.

"So we aren't going to track down who did it?" Bobbs asked.

"We'll let the FBI handle that from here on in," Meeker explained. "We pulled the general's wife out of the mess and no one seems any the wiser."

"What about the money?" Vance chimed in.

"Seems pretty clear," Meeker suggested. "Bryant was playing the role of Brown and trying to deliver what Brown was supposed to bring to the ballpark. As it wasn't in the room, the FBI must have found where it was hidden."

"I'll cut in here," Bobbs added. "Brown was O'Toole's sister. Based on the message that was in with the money, the cash was a payoff. Sometime just after Jaws gave Brown the money, she was knocked off."

"Why?" Worel asked. "Obviously they didn't get the cash."

It was Meeker's turn to pick up the story again. "It's just a guess, but I have to believe he had a score to settle with the mobster and followed him to Taylorville. It was there someone figured out who Brown was and killed her. He likely never knew about the money. I've got to believe that Bryant and Morris were in the dark as well or things would not have gone down they way they did."

"So who were the men at the ballpark?" the confused Brit asked.

"Well, the man Jaws owed was likely the man who grabbed the cash. The fact the FBI now has his body will give them an idea as to who was and who he was working for. We can tap into the President's contacts in a couple of days and find out what they know. The guy who drove off with Bryant was the bag man's partner."

"Do you have a guess as to who they are?" the Brit demanded.

"Hmm, a guess is all I have," Meeker admitted. "My first hunch is they were another crime syndicate and had done a job for the Chicago mob or they could be working for someone in law enforcement who's on the take."

"And the guys who shot the bag man?" a still curious Worel continued her probe.

"That's a mystery," Meeker admitted, "but we have a much bigger problem than figuring that out."

Barnes aimed the sedan toward a bridge crossing the Mississippi before asking the obvious? "What's that?"

"Bryant knew who I was. She called me by name."

"Does that mean the FBI knows?" the shocked driver asked.

"If Hoover had figured things out," Meeker explained, "I think the President would have known. J. Edgar would have barked at FDR for getting into to his turf. Still, there is no doubt in my mind that Bryant relished recognizing me. You could read it in her eyes and hear it in her tone … she enjoying having us face to face. And then there was some kind of cryptic bond she seemed to think we shared. She said something about us having a common secret."

"Secret?" Bobbs chimed in.

"Yeah, she said something about living forever. It just doesn't make any sense."

"But if she knows," Barnes warned, "then our undercover operation is over."

"My gut tells me she knows," Meeker noted, "but she's not sharing the information."

"But how did she find out?" Barnes demanded.

"The only source that's out there is Fister. Maybe he told her about me after Dizzy turned Fister over to her."

"So what did she do with him?" Bobbs wondered.

"That's problem number two," Meeker admitted. "It's a couple of hours to where we have the plane stored outside of Springfield. Let's pull over at the next gas station and I'll make a call to Alison. She can start using the President's contacts to dig up who knows what."

"She can also tell us if there is a time and a place for the pickup we're supposed to make in Mexico," Worel suggested.

"Yeah, that too."

A shiver went down Meeker's spine as she considered what Bryant could do to their operation. They had to find out more about her, but where would they start? She was a woman with at least three different life stories and none of them were real. She worked for the FBI and seemed to have much more trust and influence than any other woman at the Bureau. Worst of all, she appeared to be Meeker's intellectual and physical equal. For the first time since leaving Germany, the team leader was scared.

CHAPTER 22

Stanford Poole was waved past the guards at the gate of Jaws O'Toole's lake front estate. After driving up the lane, the small, thin man pulled up to the front door, switched off his 1941 Mercury's powerful V-8 engine, and slid out the door of the white coupe. After being greeted by a gorilla-sized mug named Benny, he was escorted to the study. There, sitting in a reading chair enjoying a snifter of brandy and his ever-present cigar was the man he'd come to see. The mob boss was dressed in gray slacks, a white shirt, and a burgundy smoking jacket. O'Toole's bold outfit served as quite a contrast to Poole's conservative gray suit.

"Come in Stan. Take your usual seat. Would you like something to drink?"

The visitor shook his head and eased into a leather chair. As Poole debated how to share the news of the weird episode at Sportsman's Park, O'Toole opened the conversation.

"You know, I've never asked how you got into this business. You're not exactly cut from the mold of the men who normally work in our line."

"It's not really that interesting," Poole deferred.

The host waved his expensive imported Havana cigar toward the visitor. "That's hardly true. Every person has an interesting story. The roads that we take, the turns we make, they are the reasons we end up doing what we do. Take me for instance. If I'd have stayed in Ireland, I'd have likely been a potato farmer, but instead I boxed my way to the United States. The man who managed me hooked up with a … shall we say … family business. Sometimes the family needed a bit of muscle and I quickly discovered that paid much better than boxing. Better yet, I didn't have to watch what I ate, work out or take a lot of punishment. And that's the short version of what launched me on the road to where I am today. So what brought you here?"

Poole, who'd heard O'Toole's life story a dozen times, stretched his legs out, crossed one foot over the other and shrugged, "Dumb luck."

"Explain."

"I'd just finished my college degree and was about to go to grad school when I went back to my old hometown and ran into a high school pal. He asked me to make a two-hour drive to pick something up. So I did. What I didn't realize was that he was going to withdraw some money from a bank and his collateral was his gun. So while I was sitting in the car, he shot the place up and grabbed some loot. I probably would have stayed in the clear, but we had car trouble. We were working on our sedan when a cop drove up with his wife and kid. I watched my buddy try to pick off the policemen and, in the process, the kid was shot and killed. We got into the cop's car and made our getaway. The problem was his wife was with us. My friend decided we couldn't leave any witnesses so he shot her. And even though I'd never really pulled a trigger in my whole life, there was no turning back. So I kind of figured if I were already into something, I'd better get good at it. With that in mind, I honed my skills and worked my way up until now I'm here with you."

"So," O'Toole asked, "is what happened on the fork in the road a good thing or a bad thing?"

"If you're asking would I do it again, the answer is I would've never made the trip. I think I'd have really enjoyed being married, having kids and not spending my life looking over my shoulder. But that's not the way it turned out so there's no need to squawk about it."

"You might find this hard to believe," the mobster said, his tone sincere, "but I feel kind of sorry for you."

"And I feel sorry for you, sir."

O'Toole raised his bushy eyebrows. "Why?"

"Because your sister wasn't the woman who delivered the cash at the ballpark. I have no idea who that woman was, but she didn't match the picture you gave me. Plus, everything went south in a hurry. Not only did the pickup guy have a partner, but there was another team that got involved too. What makes this group so strange was they were made up of three women and two men. I think I recognized one of them, but I can't place him right now. But don't worry, he never got a look at me. I was deep in the shadows."

The mobster took a long gulp of brandy before asking, "How did this other woman get the money?"

"Where did you leave it?"

"My sister gave me a bag. I put the cash and a note with instructions in that bag and took it to the bowling alley. After I dropped it into a rented locker, I gave the key to my sister, hung around a bit and, when I was sure no one was watching, left town."

Poole nodded. "Then someone found the key, followed your instructions, and left the bag with the pickup guy. By the way, one of my men shot and killed him when he tried to kidnap the woman. Jack thought the dame was your sister, so he can't be blamed."

"Okay, I understand. But who was the woman and how did she get the bag from my sister? I mean she wouldn't have just given it up."

"I'll try to sketch things out the way I think they happened. I stuck around in the shadows after everything broke loose. The other guy tried to make a getaway with the woman as his hostage. That's when a drop dead, auburn-haired looker raced across a parking like she was Jesse Owens and shot the guy as he drove the car. A blonde that was with her grabbed the money and before I could figure anything out, the five in that team were gone. The other dame came back over and joined another man.

By that time, a uniformed cop drove up, the guy with the dame flashed an FBI badge. With the Feds in town, I figured it was time to leave."

"So the woman pretending to be my sister was working for the Feds."

"I think that's a safe bet."

"So where's my sister?"

"Well, on the way back from St. Louis, I stopped in Taylorville. I did a little digging." Poole paused. Trying to find words was like dealing with controlling a tornado. Nothing was going to work so it was just time to shoot straight and deal with the storm that followed. "Mr. O'Toole, remember when I told you there was a murder there last week?"

"Yeah."

"Well, it was your sister who took the bullet."

As the news hung in the air, O'Toole's face suddenly grew deep red. Putting his cigar down into an ashtray, he rose from his chair and tossed the brandy glass against a far wall causing the crystal to shatter into a hundred pieces. After walking over and pounding his fist onto his desk, he screamed, "Carfano!"

"But he's dead," Poole argued.

The suddenly livid mobster turned to face his guest, his words spewing out like lead from a tommy gun. "Even though I didn't order that hit, there are some who think I did. Rudy must have told one of them about my sister and they decided to take her out as a way of payback." The big man shook his head. "If it's the last thing I do I'll find out who knocked her off and beat him to death. You heard that … I won't shoot him, I'll kill him the same way Big Al Capone did … with a baseball bat!"

It was strange scene … a man as sad as a grieving mother and as angry as wounded bull. As both of those opposite beings battled for control, O'Toole paced, cried, and cursed. Then, without warning, he stopped.

"What about the twins?"

"Twins?"

"My sister had twin girls," he explained. "What happened to my nieces?"

"They only found one girl," Poole noted. "She's in state custody. They're looking for relatives."

"I'm the only relative they have," O'Toole announced. "And where's the other twin?"

"I don't know. No one said anything about a second girl."

As the confused mobster sank into his chair, the desk phone rang.

"Get that Stan. I don't feel like talking right now."

Poole rose, strolled to the desk, leaned on the corner and, just after the third ring, picked up the receiver.

"Hello."

"Jaws, this is Darkness. Just want you to know that I have your niece. If you ever want to see her again, you better not cross me. I took out Rudy the easy way, but if you try to find out who I am or make any move against my organization, I'll take you out one piece at a time. Your sister was my way of cutting off your left arm, your niece could be the right arm if you push."

Poole looked to his boss whose head was now buried in his hands before explaining, "I'm not O'Toole. I'm just taking his messages."

"Fine, you tell him what I've told you and add this to it. I know the money was a down payment toward finding out more about me. This time, his curiosity cost him his sister. Next time it will be his niece. After that, it will be his mother in Ireland."

Poole frowned as the line went dead? Who was Darkness and how was he going to deliver the mysterious caller's message to O'Toole? A dark night had just gotten much darker.

CHAPTER 23

Wednesday, July 21, 1942
11:19 PM
In the Gulf just off the Mexico Coast

Henry Reese stood on the U-boat's deck and looked at the now inflated dingy tied alongside. His gear, the box of treasure, and a portable radio were on small craft along with two oars. Just to his right, the man who'd become his friend on this trip cracked, "Sorry we can't drop you on dry land. I guess you're going to have to paddle for about an hour before arriving in Mexico. Yet, in truth, you'll likely be moving faster than we are."

"So your vessel's in that bad of shape?" Reese asked.

"If the war lasts three years," Klein announced, "and we had a sail, we might make it back to Germany to watch the peace treaty being signed. Truthfully, it's just a matter of time before we get spotted, so it's good you're getting off now."

Reese likely should have enjoyed the thought of a German sub going down, but in this case, the commander's gloomy forecast made him a bit sad. It was never easy saying goodbye to person you liked and respected. Besides, the fact this hadn't played out as intended also meant he was not actually completing his mission. He'd been supposed to bring the great hunter in as a prisoner. As Klein's days were surely numbered and he'd likely never hunt again, that hardly seemed to matter now.

The sound of a motor caused Reese's gaze to rise from his new friend to the sky. He spotted the aircraft at the same moment the commander did. Unable to dive, the sub was a sitting duck almost completely unable to defend itself.

"You better get going," Klein yelled. He then turned to his men and called out, "Battle stations."

Jumping over the side and into the dingy, Reese pushed off into the Gulf and began to row as quickly as he could toward the shore. He was only about fifty yards away when the first shots were fired from the sub at the American fighter. Within seconds, five more aircraft appeared on the scene including two Douglas TBD-A torpedo bombers. This model plane had been nicknamed the Devastator and there was a reason. Once it dropped its payload, the results were almost always lethal. As the Grumman F4F Wildcat fighters kept the U-boat's guns busy, the Devastators' torpedoes hit the water. Twenty seconds later, the sub blew into three pieces. When the explosion struck, Klein was blown off the deck and into the Gulf.

Instincts pushed Reese to put his paddles to work heading toward the Mexican shore, but a deeper calling drew him back to the scene of the destruction. A friend floundering in the water trumped everything else at this moment. Putting his arms to work, he turned the dingy and headed back toward what was left of the German sub.

Most the U-boat's men had been below deck with their vessel blew. They had no chance. Besides the commander, the five others that had been on the deck were floating lifeless in water now surrounded by fire. So if Klein had suffered the same fate, there would be no one left to share the experiences of life on U-7071.

Pushing past pieces of metal and rowing through burning oil, Reese made it to his friend. As he floated up beside the wounded man, he set the oars to the side, reached into the water, and dragged the German into the dingy. After dropping him onto the floor, the American reversed course and headed back to the shore. Within three minutes, he was beyond the light created by the oil fire, but even though the planes could likely no longer spot him, his pace did not slow. Thirty minutes of hard rowing and five pounds of lost sweat later, he was at the beach. Leaping out, Reese pulled the dingy about thirty yards across the rocks and sand. After taking a deep breath and wiping the perspiration from his brow, he bent over to check on Klein. The commander's pulse was weak but steady. A quick examination showed burns to his right arm and back and a large bump on his head, but no bleeding. Odds were he'd make it.

Getting back to his feet, Reese dragged the inflatable off the shore and under a tree. He then pulled the radio out, turned it on and began to send out the coded message signaling where and when he was supposed to be picked up. After repeating the communication four times, he leaned back against the side of the dingy and caught his breath.

On the water, the fires were now barely glowing. In the air, the planes were still circling but no longer firing. The only thing left in this operation would be for a Coast Guard cutter to steam out about daybreak and survey the damage. It would be so easy to row out and meet that Coast Guard vessel when it showed up, but that wasn't in the cards. Doing so would blow his cover. Thus, he'd have to wait until his team arrived at the rendezvous point. That would mean at least a day of staying out of sight. Still, it was better than visiting Davy Jones's locker.

"Was ist passiert?"

Klein's question pulled Reese's gaze from the water. Turning over, he rose up on his elbows and looked into the dingy. The German's eyes were fluttering as he kept repeating the same phrase again and again. "Was ist passiert? Was ist passiert? Was ist passiert?

"The American Army Air Corps is what happened," Reese explained. "Your ship didn't stand a chance. You got hit by a couple of torpedoes."

The German nodded. "God has a sense of humor."

"What do you mean?"

"I sank a lot ships that way," he explained, "and he gave me the same treatment." He rose up to a sitting position and looked into the Gulf. "How many of my men made it?"

"You were blown clear of the fire, the rest weren't. You're the only one."

"So much for the time-honored tradition of the captain going down with his ship."

Reese recognized the sadness in Klein's tone as he spoke of not dying with his men. Most likely he would feel the guilt for the rest of his life.

"Nigel, what do we do now? Oh, and where has your British accent gone?"

Sensing it was time to end the charade, the American nodded. "My name is Henry Reese. I'm an American agent working so far undercover that only a few people in the President's office know I'm alive."

Klein smiled. "So I was right to trust you with the photo and the story."

"Yeah, your instincts were spot on."

"What happens now?"

"We wait to get picked up," Reese explained. "My team will get my coded message. They'll get here when they can and fly us back to the States."

"Us?"

"Yeah," Reese assured him, "I'm taking you with me. I figure you need to be the person to tell the President about the death camps."

"Imagine that," Klein said, "meeting Hitler and Roosevelt. Still I'm not really cut out to be a prisoner."

"Well, you could try to escape," Reese suggested. "I likely wouldn't work too hard to stop you."

"I won't if you make a promise," the German replied.

"What's that?"

"That the world thinks I'm dead. That way my family will be safe and when the war is over, I can get back to them. That is if Germany loses."

"I'll guarantee we will put the word out you're dead. And as far as your family goes, maybe the man whose identity I was supposed to share with you in exchange for the loot can arrange to smuggle them out of your country and back to the states."

"Is that possible?"

Reese sadly shook his head. "I've learned about anything is possible except peace."

"I hope's that possible too," Klein announced. "And will the woman you love be waiting for you? Will you see her again soon?"

The American shook his head. "One of them is coming to pick me up and, now that I'm safe, I'm not sure which one I really love or how I'm going to go about deciding. Who knows? I might just not love either of them."

CHAPTER 24

Thursday, July 22, 1942
12:15 AM
Team headquarters outside Drury, Maryland

Helen Meeker studied the notes laid out before her. Her sister had done a good job digging under every rock and using all of FDR's contacts, but there still was no real clue as to who Teresa Bryant really was. Beyond a résumé that didn't check out, her past was nothing more than fog.

As she looked across the table, Becca Bobbs was studying a photo. She turned it several different directions before shaking her head and frowning.

"What's wrong?" Meeker asked.

"Helen, Bryant looks familiar to me. I know I've seen her before. I just can't figure out where."

"Then," Meeker suggested, "let's play the association game. Look at the picture and tell me about the woman."

The blonde picked up the photo. "She's beautiful and exotic."

"So maybe she was a model. Maybe you've seen her in a magazine or a film?"

"No," Bobbs assured her. "It's not that."

"Okay, let's move forward. What else do you see?"

"She's strong and athletic, but I can't picture her in a sport's uniform, so that's not where I've seen her either." She paused before continuing to voice her observations. "She's dark, and it's not a tan—that is her natural skin tone. With her high cheekbones and almost black eyes, she …"

"She what?" Meeker demanded.

"This is going to sound crazy," Bobbs suggested, "but I think I know. Wait here. I've got to get a book from my room."

Once again alone, Meeker looked back at the notes. There were two things the President's contacts' information had assured her of. The first was Bryant had not shared Meeker's identity with anyone at the FBI. Roosevelt's mole there assured him that Hoover had no clue that Meeker was alive. The other thing just as revealing was that Fister was not in the Bureau's custody. So what had she done with Reggie and what game was he playing now?"

"Here it is," Bobbs announced as she marched back into the study with a large book in her hands. "And this makes no sense, so don't laugh at me. But examine the photo in chapter seven of this study of American Indian tribes and please tell me I'm not crazy."

Meeker took the book and looked at the black and white image. "You're not crazy. This has to be Bryant. That means we can at least pinpoint her tribe, which gives us a starting point for getting something on her."

Bobbs shook her head. "It's not quite that easy. The woman in that photo is named Kazwutz. She's from the Caddo Tribe. That picture was taken in 1870. If that woman's alive, she is a hundred years old or more. I'm betting Bryant is not a day over thirty-five."

"But how?"

"I don't know," the blonde chimed in, "but you're right, it at least gives us somewhere to start looking. Maybe Kazwutz was her grandmother or great grandmother and perhaps tribal records can lead us to Bryant."

Meeker laughed.

"What's so funny?"

"Bryant wondered if I'd learned her secret of living forever."

"I'm not buying that," Bobbs announced, "but I am buying she's an American Indian."

"You birds clucking for a reason?" Gail Worel inquired as she entered the room.

"I can see you're ready for bed," Meeker noted. "Nice robe."

"Military issue," the Englishwoman explained as she looked down at the drab, gray wrap, "and it's not very soft. So have you figured anything out?"

The ringing phone interrupted Bobbs' explanation of what they did and mostly didn't know. As she and Worel looked on, Meeker answered.

"Who is this?"

"Alison. The package you're supposed to pick up has arrived."

"Are you speaking in slang or is this a straight message?"

"Straight."

"Okay, where and when?"

"Rio Largartos. The package will be expecting you in Jose's at noon. I'm guessing that is hotel, a bar, or a cafe. They will be there every day at that time until you arrive."

"We'll leave tomorrow and, if all goes well, meet them on Friday."

"Take care, sis."

"Thanks. I love you and will see you soon."

Meeker set the phone down and looked over to the other two. "The package has finally been delivered. It's in a Mexican town named Rio Lorgartos. So, Gail, you're about to get those jewels back and see the man who's so special to you."

"About time," came the response.

"Who's going?" Bobbs asked.

"We'll leave Dizzy here and load up."

"Maybe you need to stay here too," the blonde suggested.

"Why?"

"To get more information on Bryant."

"Dizzy can worked with Alison and do that," Meeker announced. "I don't want to miss Gail's reaction when she sees her man. I'm thinking the British reserve will melt in a real hurry."

"Well," Bobbs suggested, "maybe neither of us needs to invade that moment. Perhaps it would be best if we stayed here and Dizzy and Clay served as the escorts."

"Come on, Becca, you're always up for some adventure. Besides, there might be some fireworks and, if so, we'll need to be there to provide some cover. There are rumored to be German operatives in Mexico. If they get wind of this, they'll descend on this place too."

The blonde nodded, but still didn't look happy.

"Okay," Meeker barked. "Alert Clay and Dizzy, pack enough for a couple of days, and let's see if we can take off around sunup. Before then, let's grab a few hours of sleep." As she strolled out of the study, Meeker called out, "Sweet dreams! And, Gail, I'm never going to forgive you if this guy doesn't live up to the picture you've painted of him."

Don't forget the previous episodes ...
In the President's Service Series.

More from Ace Collins.

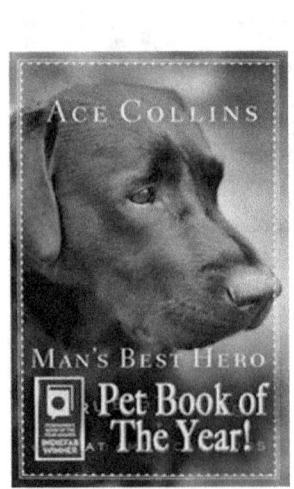